THE LATE HUSBAND

CHASITY BOWLIN

The Vanishing of Lord Vale

The Missing Marquess of Althorn

The Resurrection of Lady

The Mystery of Miss Mason

The Awakening of Lord Ambrose

Hyacinth

A Midnight Clear

The Pirate's Bluestocking (A Pirates of Britannia Crossover)

THE VICTORIAN GOTHIC COLLECTION

House of Shadows

Veil of Shadows

Passage of Shadows

THE HELLION CLUB SERIES

A Rogue to Remember

Barefoot in Hyde Park

What Happens In Piccadilly

Sleepless In Southampton

When An Earl Loves A Governess (coming soon)

The Duke's Magnificent Obsession

The Governess Diaries

THE LYON'S DEN CONNECTED WORLD

Fall Of The Lyon

Tamed By The Lyon

THE WYLDE WALLFLOWERS

One Wylde Night

A Kiss Gone Wylde (coming soon)

Too Wylde To Tame (coming soon)

Wylde At Heart (coming soon)

Chapter One

Her small shop just off Bond Street was bustling. It was the eve of the social season, after all, and all the managing mamas launching their daughters into the marriage market were looking to see their debutantes outfitted to the nines.

"Good heavens! I've never seen the like!"

The exclamation had come from Bridget, her shop girl. There was a team of seamstresses working in a small room in the back to create the garments that would make some girls the toast of the Ton and others a laughingstock. She only gave them what they asked for, after all. Guide them as she might toward a more refined and flattering gown, she could not force them to have good taste or the sense to know what looked good on them in some cases.

Pursing her lips, Sabine de Roussard replied, "Oui, oui. It is tres…bizzee!" She put extra emphasis on the last word, lifting the 'e' sound in an exaggerated accent. She didn't need anyone to believe she was actually French, after all. She just needed to be certain no one recognized her as being from Yorkshire.

Bridget nodded. "Will we need to take on another seamstress? I've got a cousin, just come up from the country, who is a fine hand with needle and thread."

Sabine looked around. "Oui. Have her come tomorrow morning and bring a sample of her work. I will decide if she is up to zee standard."

It was completely overdone. She knew it. Even Bridget, a girl born and bred in the rookeries, looked askance at her. She was not Sabine de Roussard, though she longed to be. Having been born Sally Barker and having the great misfortune to marry Lawrence Russell, a heavy-handed and cruel mill owner, Sabine de Roussard was the identity she had created for herself when she left him bleeding on the floor of their bedchamber and fled to London.

The bell above the door tinkled, and a small boy entered. Sabine recognized him immediately as a stable lad. More particularly, she recognized him as a stable lad in the employ of the Earl of Winburn. Edmund Grayson—or Gray, as he preferred to be called—had returned. Nearly ten long days he'd been gone to the countryside to deal with an estate matter. Ten days of not being held in his arms, of not being kissed by his perfect lips or reveling in the exquisite pleasure he could ring from her body.

Had anyone told her that she would ever welcome a man into her bed after her late husband's cruelty, much less that she would do so with unrepentant enthusiasm, she would have thought them mad. As the boy approached her, holding out a folded slip of paper, she pulled a coin from the pocket of her apron and deposited it in his hand. "Merci."

The boy accepted his coin and scampered away. He would likely go to the sweet shop a few doors down and spend it all on candies. But little boys in service so rarely got treats such as that, so she would not bother to warn or scold him. Instead, Sabine opened the missive.

It was not a love letter; that was not his way. Some women might have been offended by the terseness of it, but she was not. It had been likely dashed off as he walked through the doors, stripping his mud-splattered coat as he went.

Tonight. Eight o'clock.

—G

She didn't even consider saying no or pretending that she had other plans. She would be there in the townhouse he had insisted she reside in. The townhouse that, at her last birthday, he had gifted to her outright. It was an extravagant gesture, and she'd protested, but he'd said something that halted her words.

"I want to know that I am here because you desire my presence. Not because my name is on the lease."

And she did desire his presence. Beyond anything else, she longed to be near him, so much so that it terrified her. But not enough to make her quit him entirely. She didn't think there was a power on Earth that could do that.

"Bridget, I will be late in zee morning... You will open zee shop, no?"

Bridget smirked. "Aye, Madame. I will."

The girl was impertinent, but Sabine decided not to remark on it. Bridget was very timely, tidy, and dependable. She was also completely trustworthy. Those qualities were in short supply.

Glancing at the small clock on her worktable, she noted that it was just after two in the afternoon. She was willing the hours away until she could dash out to go and meet him.

———

GRAY WASN'T in the best of moods. Seated in a tub of steaming water, washing the muck of the road from his flesh, his musings turned to the source of his disquiet. They were numerous. An estate manager who had been siphoning funds had been dealt with, but a replacement had not yet been found. The tenants whose roofs had not been repaired and whose rents had been reported as being late when in fact they had gone into the estate manager's pockets, those were all issues still to be sorted out. Then there was his other issue: Sabine. If that was even her name. He knew it likely was not.

The woman had been like a fire in his blood from the moment he'd met her. It had been more than a year ago when they'd first crossed paths. His sister had been in town and required a new dress. He didn't know why. In his mind, women always seemed to need a new dress for something. She'd convinced him to accompany her on her errands that day, to escort her to her new dressmaker and then to retrieve her there when the appointment was complete. When he'd entered that shop, his gaze had been immediately drawn to the dark-haired beauty who had been wrapping a parcel for his sister.

Sabine de Roussard, the little placard next to the door had read. Wearing a dress of deep-green silk, with a simple ribbon tied about her slender throat, there had been no doubt that she was the dressmaker. A shop girl would not have been dressed so fine. And from that moment forward, he had pursued her. It had taken months to lure her to his bed. In those months, he'd discovered some unnerving truths about her.

The first truth was that she was not French. He was convinced, in fact, that she barely spoke French, and if she'd ever stepped foot outside of England, he would eat his hat. The second truth was thatr her life, whatever it had been before she gifted herself with the moniker of Madame de Roussard, had not been an easy one. Someone, somewhere along the way, had hurt her deeply. Beneath the silk that always graced her body, there were vicious scars that hinted at the violence in her past. The third and most disturbing truth was perhaps more about himself than about her: He loved her. Deeply. To the breadth and depths of his soul, he loved her. So much so that he was willing to brave the censure of his peers to make her his wife. He would have asked already if he had a hope in hell of her saying yes. But he knew she would refuse him. The question was *why*. Would she say no because she didn't love him in return? He didn't think so. He was fairly certain her feelings were in accord with his own. Would she say no to him because of their very different social positions? Perhaps. Would she reject him because she feared her violent past might one day catch up to her? That, he thought, was the most likely answer. But he'd never know for certain until he was brave enough to pose the question.

Cursing, he gave his hair one final, cursory scrub before dumping an ewer of water over his head to rinse the soap from it. Then he rose and grabbed the drying cloth draped over a chair nearby. Draping it about his waist, he walked to the window and stared out. As he did so, he saw the young stable lad hurrying back through the mews. He carried a paper-wrapped parcel in his hands. No doubt Sabine had given him a coin and the lad had spent it on candies.

Gray started to turn away, but another figure, further down the lane, caught his eye. A man stepped from the shadowy recesses between two buildings. His eyes were trained on the young boy, watching him in such a way that it was impossible not to feel the menace emanating from him. Who was he? What did he want?

Gray decided they would no longer use the young stable lad as their messenger. The boy would be disappointed, but that was far better than him being hurt. There were villains enough about that would readily and eagerly exploit a young child. He would not do anything to place the lad in harm's way. It might not be amiss to have a word with the stable master and coachman if they happen to see anyone lurking about.

At that moment, his valet entered the bathing chamber. "Will you be dining at your club this evening, my lord? Or shall I inform the staff you intend to dine at home?"

"I have a private engagement, Lawton," Gray replied. "Informal. The blue superfine, doeskin breeches and riding boots shall suffice. Lay them out and I will dress myself."

The valet sighed, world weary and put upon. "Yes, my lord. Will you require my assistance shaving?"

He considered it, but then he thought of just how

Sabine shivered when he ran his whiskered chin over her skin. "No. There's no need. That will be all, Lawton."

"Shall you require my assistance upon your return, my lord?"

Gray didn't snap at him, but it was a near thing. The man was like an old mother hen. "No, Lawton. I shall be returning late, and I am uncertain of the hour. There is no need for you to wait. Enjoy an evening of leisure for a change, won't you? Have a drink. Read a book, for heaven's sake."

"It is not my half day, my lord."

"I'm giving you another half day," Gray said, his tone sharper than intended. "Just go, Lawton. I am in a foul mood and best left to my own devices."

The valet gathered up the discarded clothing. "Yes, my lord. Good evening to you."

Alone, Gray turned back to the window and stared down at the spot where the shady character had been lurking. He was gone, having either slunk back to his hiding place or left for good. Which, he could not say. But something about the incident plagued him, and for the life of him he couldn't figure out why.

Chapter Two

It was just after seven when Sabine managed to scramble into what was considered a modest town-house in Mayfair. In the rest of the world, it was positively palatial. It certainly was by any standard which she had previously lived.

Climbing the stairs quickly, she called out for the maid to bring water for washing. She did not have an overabundance of servants in the house, preferring as much privacy as possible. Of course, many servants would also turn up their nose at working for a woman such as herself. It didn't matter that she was a nobleman's mistress. No. It had much more to do with the fact that she was in trade. Something about making dresses for ladies struck them as being less respectable than taking off her dress for a gentleman. What a strange world they lived in that even the servants were snobs.

Reaching her chamber, exquisitely furnished with a large tester bed draped in dark-green velvet, she began stripping off the dress she'd worn for work. She didn't bother selecting another from her wardrobe. Instead, she chose a simple chemise of fine lawn and lace, along with a wrapper in pale peach silk, and laid them across the bed. It was a ridiculous garment, but it had been a gift from Gray. He'd even remarked on how damned odd it was to buy her clothes when she was one of the finest dressmakers in London. He'd told her he knew that because at every function he attended, he heard ladies remarking on where they'd gotten this gown or the other. Of course, as she'd told him, it was a luxury for her to wear something she had not made herself.

Leaving those garments on the bed, she took the pins from her hair and let the mass of it fall down over her shoulders. Then she brushed it till it shone. It would be something she would regret the following morning, leaving it down. But he preferred it. And she loved the way he looked at her when he saw it. The hunger in his gaze never failed to ignite her own desire. Not that it took so very much with him. A glance. A simple touch. Sometimes, just watching the almost animalistic grace of his movements as he crossed the room was enough to make her want to simply throw herself at him.

The maid entered then, carrying a large pitcher of hot water. With her reverie about Gray's many charms interrupted, Sabine quickly discarded the remainder of her garments and began to wash. When she was done, she applied a small amount of the perfume from her dressing table. It, too, had also been a gift from him. With her evening toilette complete, she donned the carefully selected garments just as the maid returned to retrieve her soiled ones.

"Will you be dining with company tonight, ma'am?"

"Yes. The earl will be arriving at eight. I completely forgot to ask what cook had prepared."

"A note was sent round earlier from the earl's house. Cook prepared a cold supper of meat, cheese and bread. I'll bring it up shortly with some wine and put it in the sitting room."

Their affair was like a well-orchestrated military campaign, she thought. Between errand boys, cooks, maids, valets, and butlers, she wondered if there was a soul left in London that didn't know what they were about. "That's perfect, Hazel. Thank you."

"Yes, ma'am. Will you be needing anything else?"

"No, Hazel. That will be all. The earl will let himself in."

The maid nodded, bobbed a curtsy, and departed.

Alone, Sabine made her way to the small sitting room just beyond her bedchamber. A fire had been lit, the blaze cheerily dancing to ward off the cool of the evening. Picking up the novel she had been attempting to read in her free hours, she turned to the last page she'd read. But she stared at it, not seeing the words. She couldn't think of anything but him.

Moments later, Hazel reentered the room, bearing the dinner tray. She placed it on the table just as heavy footfalls sounded on the stairs. The maid bobbed another quick curtsy and exited hastily.

Closing her book, Sabine waited. Seconds later, he entered. His broad frame filled the doorway, his dark hair a tad too long and pushed back off his forehead. It would fall forward again. And when he slept, it would look almost boyish but for the hard planes and angles of a face that was rugged and handsome beyond measure.

"Welcome home, my lord," she said, her accent slipping a bit.

"Your English is improving," he noted with a grin.

It was a ruse that they both played along with.

"I have many opportunities to practice in my shop with all the ladies of the Ton. One or two have even discussed you, my lord. The marriage mart has opened, and you are eligible, no?"

He stepped deeper into the room, removing his coat and draping it over a chair. His cravat came next, the simple knot sliding free and the silk slipping between his fingers to be discarded there also. "No. I am not eligible. There will be no debutantes. No marriage-minded mamas. No betrothals to any of those simpering chits. I have removed myself from the marriage mart permanently."

She smiled, though her heart sang in relief. It hadn't been jealousy that prompted her to ask, but self protection. A time would come when he would need a wife. And while she was his mistress, she would not be the sort to share. At that point, she would have to let him go. It pained her to even think it.

"That is good to hear. I would hate to think of you rushing from my bed to your wife's."

He unbuttoned his waistcoat and slipped it off, tossing it aside so carelessly that it landed in a crumpled heap on the floor.

"I have a light supper for us," she said.

"Later. Much later. There are other needs to be met first," he replied, a slight growl to his voice.

Shivering slightly in response, Sabine rose to her feet. "I've missed you." There was no hint of the fake French accent. Some things, when said, should not be tainted with artifice.

"And I've missed you," he said. Devoid of everything but his breeches and riding boots, he closed the distance between them and swept her into his arms.

He kissed her like a man starved, his lips moving hungrily over hers in a way that left her breathless and clinging to him desperately. It seemed as if her wrapper and chemise simply melted beneath the heat of his hands. The garments were gone in a whisper, leaving her naked in his arms.

They did not reach the comfort of her bed. Instead, he settled on the settee and drew her down to sprawl over his lap. Feeling his powerful thighs beneath her and the hard ridge of his arousal pressed firmly against her, Sabine didn't hesitate. She reached between them, freeing the button fall of his breeches. Taking him in her hand, feeling the silken skin of his shaft beneath her fingertips, she rose on her knees. It was all the invitation he needed.

As she lowered herself, he was gliding into her, filling her with such perfection that her eyes fluttered closed, and a pleasured cry escaped her lips. For just a moment, she went utterly still and savored that blissful sensation. Then she began to rock, her hips moving in an ancient rhythm as his hands and lips coasted over her skin with a kind of reverence and gentleness that belied the biting, clawing nature of the need they both felt.

It did not take long for her to reach the pinnacle of her pleasure, to hover there on that precipice. Arching her back, she took him deeper, even as she sank down upon him one last time. Her breath hissed out between clenched teeth and her body quaked with the intensity of her release. And he held her close, his own hips straining beneath her as he took his pleasure as well.

With their breath still ragged, he shook his head. "That was rather disappointingly brief."

"Only if we're finished," she answered, letting her head drop onto his shoulder.

"Not even close. Ten days is too long to be without you."

One day was too long, she thought. But saying so would leave her too vulnerable. So, she remained quiet and enjoyed the sensation of his heart thumping beneath her cheek as she snuggled against the firm wall of his chest. His arms closed about her, holding her there as his fingers tangled in the loose strands of her hair. It was comfortable. Not in a boring way, but in an easy way. She didn't hide her scars. She didn't mind if her atrocious accent slipped entirely in his presence. He never pressed her for answers. Not because he didn't want them. She knew that. But he'd told her once that he would hear them when she was ready to share them. And that was how it had been with them from the beginning. There was nothing that created greater intimacy than the complete acceptance of one another—faults, secrets and all.

Chapter Three

Gray awoke in the last minutes before dawn. Pale silver light seeped between the drawn curtains. He was content enough to be awake but was far from ready to get out of the warm bed and leave the soft, warm body that was pressed against him. With her dark hair spilling about the both of them, he'd likely never manage to get up without waking her anyway.

Staring up at the velvet-draped canopy, he thought about the question he'd wanted to pose to her. The question that, somehow, he'd not found the right time to ask her last night. Of course, they had been enthusiastically and repeatedly engaging in other very pleasant activities. He also knew he would likely not receive the answer he wanted.

It had been on his mind a great deal of late. But ten days in the country—ten long days without seeing her, touching her, or hearing her voice—had finally cemented for him one undeniable truth. Not that he loved her. That, he'd known for months now. It was, quite simply, that he would likely never love anyone else the way that he loved her. Nor would he ever need another person as he needed her. He craved her every moment of every day, and not just her wanton and energetic response to his lovemaking. No. He craved her company, her presence, her affection.

"I can hear you thinking," she said sleepily, as she draped one leg over his thigh and placed her hand on his opposite hip.

"Minx," he muttered. "You've done me in."

She raised up on her elbow and stared down at him with a saucily raised eyebrow. "I seem to recall you instigating our amorous activities a time or two."

"Three," he corrected with a grin.

She rolled away from him and rose from the bed, heedless of her nudity. At one point in time, she would have shied away from such a display. She'd have kept her wrapper at the ready to hide the vicious scars that marked her body. Now, in the pale morning light, he could see them in stark relief. He knew what they were. At some time in her life, someone had flogged the beautiful woman before him. They'd whipped her until she bled, leaving deep gouges in the flesh of her back and shoulders. There were other scars, but it was those on her back that caused a visceral reaction in him. He wanted to find the person who had done it and visit that same treatment upon them.

"I have to be at the shop this morning. I have several very prestigious clients coming in, and they will be most put out if they must deal with a simple shop girl rather than Madame de Roussard herself," she explained.

There was a hint of Yorkshire in her voice then. It often crept out in the early mornings or late at night, when she was very tired. "You do not have to be Madame de Roussard. You could retire quite comfortably from your profession."

"And do what?" she asked, picking up her hairbrush and tackling the snarls in her hair.

It was the opportunity he'd been waiting for. "Being a countess, I'm told, keeps one very busy."

The hairbrush clattered to the floor. She stood there, blinking at him for a moment, before turning away, her movements jerky with anger and shock. "You've gone entirely mad. What a horrid thing to jest about!"

Gray sat up in bed, his gaze locked on her. "It isn't a jest, Sabine. I've a ring in my coat pocket, topped with a sapphire the size of a robin's egg. I'd put it on your finger today if you'd let me," he said.

"Is this how you propose? Really?" She said it offhandedly, but her voice trembled just a bit, just enough to reveal how deeply upset she was over it all.

"No," he answered. "It isn't a proposal. This is how I tell you that I want to marry you. I want nothing more than to wake up every morning, for the rest of our lives, with you by my side. But I will not ask until I know that you are free to say yes or no of your own accord. I know you well enough to know that sometimes you need to mull an idea over for a time before being asked to make a decision."

"There is no decision, Gray. I cannot marry you," she replied.

"Cannot or will not?" It was an important distinction for him.

Silence descended as she carefully considered how to respond. At last, she offered, "Cannot."

"Because of our difference in stations or because of something in your very secret past?"

She turned back to him then, facing him. There were unshed tears in her eyes, hovering on her dark lashes. "Both, really. If I had to weigh them, I would say it is the latter more than the former which impacts my stance on the matter."

"You have a husband, then." It was something he'd wondered about often. Given her scars, if she'd run from the bastard who put them on her to start with, no one in their right mind could blame her. But the law did not see it that way. By rights, she was the property of a husband, even if the husband was a sadistic bastard.

"I was married," she answered carefully. "It was a

lifetime ago. I won't say more about it than that. I can't."

He considered her very cagey response and countered accordingly. "There are few things in this world that a sufficient amount of money and a sufficient amount of power cannot overcome. Remember that, Sabine. And remember that no matter what occurs, you will always be mine."

"I'm not owned by any man. Never again."

"It isn't about ownership, unless we own each other. It's about the fact that you're a part of me now. You've taken up residence in my very soul, I think. And for better or worse, I've grown accustomed to your presence there."

SABINE SAID nothing further as he rose from the bed and began locating his scattered articles of clothing. She loved him with a kind of desperation that she honestly resented. It was the very antithesis of everything she'd set out to secure in her life—independence, autonomy, freedom. And yet she felt tied to him like a ship anchored in a harbor. She might drift a bit here and there, but she'd never go far, because he held her steady, safe and secure. But like an anchored ship, a storm could wreck it all. And there were storms in her past, far more than he realized and some so ugly they might alter everything, including how he felt about her.

How did one tell one's lover that they were a murderess? It wasn't possible. She'd left her last husband, Lawrence Russell, bleeding profusely on the floor of their bedchamber as she'd run for her life. It hadn't been coldblooded or premeditated. The situation had been volatile, and if she hadn't acted as she had, he would have certainly killed her. But English law favored a husband who murdered his wife, while wives who murdered their husbands only met one fate —the noose.

She doubted that Gray would be able to save her from that fate if the truth ever came out. Even if he could, what would it cost him? What would it alter in their relationship? She could never move freely in society for fear of running into her late husband's acquaintances. But as a dressmaker… Well, no one ever looked at the help, did they? She might as well be invisible to the ladies who frequented her shop, so long as she offered them quality merchandise and did so in a timely manner.

But, as they stood there in the dim morning light, the wreckage of his declaration littered about them, she felt she owed him something. So, she said all that she could. "I wish it were different… That I had met you first. If I had, well, who knows where we'd be today?"

He glanced back at her. "I'm not one for looking at the past and wishing it away. It forged you, didn't it? You are the woman you are—the woman I love—because of all that you've endured. There's nothing I'd change about you except your situation. If you ever choose to be free of the past that haunts you, I will move heaven and earth to make it happen."

"This sounds an awfully lot like a goodbye," she said, her voice catching on a sob that she choked back.

"It isn't," he said softly. "I'm not strong enough for that. But I might need a day or two to lick my wounded pride."

"It wounds your pride that I said no?"

"It wounds my pride that you don't have enough faith in my ability to protect you to say yes. But I shall endure it," he replied. Having retrieved his breeches and donned them, he closed the distance between them and took her in his arms.

Sabine leaned into him, savoring that sensation. It was all the more precious to her because, for a moment, she had thought such gestures would be gone from her forever. "It isn't that I do not trust you. It's that the things in my life that I've run away from are far uglier than you could ever imagine. Don't let this come between us. Please."

"For now, it won't. But we both know a day will come when what we have right now is not enough," he warned.

She would deal with that when the time came. For the moment, she simply pressed her face to his chest and held on.

23

Chapter Four

Sabine made her way to the shop. It was a different sort of crowd on the Mayfair streets at that time of morning. Servants, delivery men, butchers, bakers, and all the assorted tradesmen who made life within the hallowed walls of those stately homes bearabley were all about, bustling to and fro. For herself, she blended in. Those were her people, after all. In another life, years earlier, she might have been one of the ladies lying in bed, being served chocolate and toast while she lounged in her nightclothes and considered who might pay a call to her that day or whom she herself might visit.

It felt like someone else, she realized. All those years ago, being part of the social circle in Yorkshire, calling on her peers even as she seated herself gingerly on the chair to avoid the sting of fresh bruises doled out by her husband the night before. Every moment of her life had been a study in pretense or terror and pain. There had been nothing else. She might have smiled and laughed or made polite conversation with those around her, but in her mind, she'd been dreading what was to come or reliving what had already taken place.

Even now, years after the fact, she often found herself looking over her shoulder, expecting to catch a glimpse of the man who'd made her every waking hour a living hell. The thought seemed to conjure the action. Almost against her will, Sabine glanced behind her.

At first, she thought it was her imagination, a waking nightmare to torment her. Lawrence Russell stood on the corner, next to one of the gated entrances to Hyde Park. He wore a black cloak, as had always been his habit. He held his hat in a gloved hand, and even from a distance, she could see the wicked scar at his temple. Her steps faltered, and she stumbled and fell, her knees cracking against the paved sidewalk. A carriage rumbled past, and a helpful shopgirl assisted her to her feet. Sabine looked back, and he was gone—if he'd ever been there at all.

"Are you all right, ma'am? You look like you've seen a ghost!" the shopgirl said.

"I'm quite all right," Sabine reassured her. "Thank you for your assistance."

"'Tis a shame about your dress. What lovely, fine silk!"

Glancing down, Sabine saw the tears in the fabric just at her knee. She could see the paler fabric of her petticoat beneath. "A bit of artfully placed embroidery should mend it nicely. Thank you again, Miss…"

"Watson, ma'am. Merrilee Watson. Formerly of Buxcom's Millinery. He sacked me this morning for telling a lady not to buy a hat."

"Why would you tell a customer not to buy a hat?"

"Because it looked dreadful on her. I tried to steer her towards one that would be better suited to her, but he wouldn't have none of it. Told her I was a country girl with no eye for fashion and sent me packing," Merilee Watson said with a shake of her head.

"Then you shall come work for me, Merilee Watson. I have never fired a girl for telling zee truth," Sabine added with a flourish of her fake accent. "I am Madame de Roussard."

The girl's mouth dropped open. "Oh, I've heard of you! Everyone talks about your gowns!"

"Come along, Merilee. We shall walk togezzer," Sabine stated, and linked arms with the girl. It wasn't entirely a gesture of gratitude for her help. It gave her a false sense of security, not being alone after the vision she'd had. Had it been real? Had Lawrence really been there? But mhe was supposed to be dead. She'd been told by Mrs. Atkins that he was dead. Why on earth would the woman have lied to her?

She needed answers, and she needed them immediately. But, first, she needed to see Merilee settled with Bridget and training to help in the shop, and then she needed to see to the hiring of Bridget's cousin for piece work. What a morning it had been!

As they neared Bond Street, Sabine glanced behind her once more. There was no dark, familiar figure there. There were no ghosts from her past. Only the fear remained, and that would stay with her for quite a long time to come.

STANDING behind a tall hedge in Hyde Park, he smiled wickedly to himself, having finally confirmed once and for all that he'd found the right woman. He'd been watching her for days. There was no question it was her. He'd known it was Sally from the very moment he'd laid eyes on her. She was his wife, after all. *Mrs. Lawrence Russell.* Calling herself Sabine de Roussard couldn't hide her true identity, and her phony French accent couldn't entirely hide the York-shire in her voice.

But there were differences. Her figure was fuller, for one. She'd put on weight. It grudged him to admit that it suited her. But the biggest change was her demeanor. She didn't act like his wife anymore. This was no timid waif who cowered and covered her face. This woman was bold as brass and immoral to boot. He'd seen her lover coming and going from her house. He'd watched the boy deliver the note to her yesterday and had followed him back. The Earl of Winburn. She'd whored herself for the favor of a titled gentleman. But, to his mind, all women were whores. Some simply had higher prices than others.

It hadn't taken much digging to unearth the gossip about her, once he'd known what name she used. A chance encounter had spoiled her new identity. A serving girl had accompanied her mistress to a dress shop on a London excursion. That same serving girl had worked briefly in his home as a maid and had seen the portrait of the missing and presumed dead Mrs. Russell. Of course, there had still been a modest reward posted for any information about her whereabouts, living or dead.

The story he'd told to explain her disappearance and to explain away the vicious head wound he'd received that night had been a simple one. They'd left the ball at the local assembly rooms earlier than expected. In so doing, they'd surprised a burglar who had been looting their home for jewels and valuables. The brigand had knocked him unconscious and left him for dead, bleeding like a stuck pig before stealing away Mrs. Russell with the intent to ransom her back to anyone that would pay. And, later on, the imaginary villain had reconsidered his plan, murdered the poor soul, and left her body to rot in a shallow grave, possibly never to be found. The lie had been convenient at the time, but no longer. Now, with his textile mills failing, he needed cash. He needed another wealthy wife.

If he had her arrested, she would hang for what she'd done. But telling the truth—that his slip of a wife had bashed him in the head with a poker and nearly ended his life—was an indignity he would never admit to. But he wouldn't have to now. He had found her. He didn't intend to drag her back to Yorkshire to face justice for her crimes. He didn't intend to drag her back at all. He intended to complete the job he'd begun that night and see the bitch dead. She would pay for what she'd done to him, and when he could prove her death, he would be free to marry again, this time to an heiress of much more liberal fortune.

Lawrence nodded to himself, well satisfied with the day's work. He had the lay of the land. He knew what route she took to and from her little shop. He knew how her lover communicated with her and arranged their assignations. It was all he needed in order to lure her to a spot where he could end her miserable existence once and for all. As he walked away, he began to whistle a jaunty tune.

Chapter Five

Gray dimmed his fingers atop his desk, lost in thought. What was it in her past that she feared so much? He didn't doubt the ugliness of it. Her scars were proof enough, after all. But that she still had so much fear of it in the present could mean only one of two things: first, that whoever was responsible for her suffering could still be after her and, second, that she'd done something illegal in her past and had to hide from potential consequences.

"…and I hesitate to say it, my lord, but I very much fear you will have to bring the man to trial. The amount of money he has siphoned from the estate is considerable. I doubt you'll recoup any of the losses, but he should certainly be made to pay for his crimes."

Realizing that he'd not heard half of what his solicitor had said, Gray pulled his hand back from the desk, ending his interminable drumming—a habit that had begun to annoy him, as well. "No. I dislike the attention it would draw, and I've no wish to have everyone in society whispering about my inability to differentiate between hardworking employees and criminals. I'd rather suffer the cost than deal with the scandal." Especially since, if he had his way and married Sabine, that scandal would rock all of London. No point in shaking it up twice, after all.

"Are you certain, sir?" the solicitor questioned. "It is a great deal of money."

"Will taking him to court recoup any of it?" Gray demanded.

"I would think it unlikely, sir. I do believe, based on what our investigators discovered, that the man has a penchant for gambling and possesses far more enthusiasm than skill."

"Then, I'm certain," Gray stated firmly. But even then, an idea was forming. He ought to dismiss it out of hand. There was no way that, if it were discovered, he would be forgiven for such encroachment. Yet, he had to know, for her sake as well as his own. "Our investigators, Smythe…how discreet can they be?"

"As discreet as you desire, my lord."

"I need information about Madame de Roussard. She has only been in town a few years, but I'd like to discover where she was prior to that—and not that cocked-up story about her being the daughter of emigres. I want the truth of it. I fear digging into her past could create difficulties for her, and that should be avoided at all costs. I want the truth, without alerting anyone who would or could mean her harm. Can that be done?"

Smythe scratched his balding head. "It's a complex situation, my lord. If it can be done, then it would be Hatton and his crew that could do it. I certainly wouldn't entrust such a mission to anyone else."

"Put them on it," Gray ordered. "Urge caution and extreme discretion. And at the first hint of a problem, I am to be notified immediately. Is that clear?"

"Yes, my lord. Might I ask why this is a necessity now when you've been entertaining the lady in question for over a year already? Is there something I should be aware of?"

Gray could hear the disapproval in the other man's voice. "If there is, at any time, something I should tell you, Smythe, then I will do so. If you've anything further to add on the subject, I would remind you that solicitors are thick on the ground in London, and it would be easy enough to find one who is not so free with opinions."

Subdued, Smythe nodded in the most obsequious manner that Gray had ever observed in the man. "Certainly, my lord. I have no opinion unless it is your wish for me to do so. I shall be off, if you require nothing else."

"No, nothing else today. Let me know the moment Hatton finds something."

"Yes, my lord. Good day, sir."

With the solicitor gathering up his things to go, Gray returned to his less-than-peaceful ruminations. He hadn't actually thought she would agree. It had never entered his mind that he would broach the subject of marriage with her and she would simply fall in line with his wishes. He had known it would be a battle. But he had expected to battle her rationales about their differences in station, about her business, even about her desire for independence and no wish to be married at all. He hadn't expected to battle her fear. And it was fear that he'd seen in her eyes. When she'd mentioned her past, albeit briefly, he'd seen a kind of terror in her that he never wished to witness again. Whatever it was that held her back, she feared it more than she loved him. And he knew she loved him. Sabine de Roussard, if that was even her name, was not the sort of woman who would be any man's mistress without her heart being involved.

It had been months of wooing to even get her there. Months of quiet dinners, of long, drugging kisses. He'd gifted her with jewels, and she'd smiled in thanks because, while she appreciated their beauty, they were not something she desired above all else. He'd plucked a flower from the garden and placed it her hair, and she had wept. She was a woman who appreciated gentleness, and having seen her scars, he could readily understand why.

He knew her. He knew her mind, her heart, her soul. But he likely did not know her name. Her past was entirely a blank to him, save for the glossy and utterly false tale about being the daughter of French émigrés, a tailor and his wife who had been a dressmaker in the royal court. It was practiced, well rehearsed, and utterly false. Her mother might have been a dressmaker, or her father might have been a tailor, but if they had been, it had happened in Yorkshire.

Smythe had just shoved the last document into his leather satchel when Gray stopped him. "Tell Hatton to start in Yorkshire. Any dressmakers or tailors with daughters who are missing or dead."

"Yorkshire?" Smythe asked. "I thought she was French."

"Clearly, you've no ear for languages. If she's bloody French, then so am I."

"And she's been concealing it from you all this time?"

"Hardly. Anyone who has even a passing acquaintance with French will know within the pronunciation of the first word from Madame de Roussard that she has never set foot across the channel," Gray stated with amusement. "I do not think she cares to convince people she's from France as much as she wishes to disguise the fact that she's from Yorkshire. That's telling for me. Get them on it. At once."

Smythe nodded again, hoisted his satchel onto his shoulder and left the study.

Gray reached into his coat pocket and retrieved the small leather box. Opening the latch on it, he flipped back the lid and stared at the ring inside. The gold band was heavily ornamented, carved with a looping vine pattern. The large cabochon sapphire was ringed with smaller alternating diamonds and pearls. It was a thing of beauty. It had been in his family for several generations, reworked, added to and dressed up over the years, but the stone itself had been gifted by a maharaja to his great grandfather in India. It wasn't the value of the stone that mattered to him; he wanted to see it on her finger because it had been worn by every bride in his direct line since his great grandfather had it set and gifted it to his new bride.

There was nothing he wanted more than to slide that ring on her finger. He wanted the world to know that she was his. More importantly, he wanted her to know that, whatever their difference in their stations or background, he was proud to love her and be loved by her. In all his life, he'd never been so close to a person as he was to her. There was a vulnerability that occurred in loving someone so completely, so wholly. He had never experienced anything like it. It was both terrifying and exhilarating.

With a muttered curse, he flipped the lid closed on the box, latched it, and slid it back into his pocket. He could stare at it all day, and it wouldn't change a damn thing. Reaching for the quill on his desk, he dashed off a short note and rang for a footman. When the servant entered, he handed him the missive. "Deliver that to Madame de Roussard's shop on Bond Street. Immediately."

He wouldn't be seeing her in her home that night. He had something else in mind, but it would require careful planning and execution. With that, he called for his butler. No one but Hinton could accomplish all that needed to be done in such a short time.

Chapter Six

It was a rarity that she would leave her shop early two days in a row. In fact, it was a rarity that she would leave her shop early at all. But another missive had arrived from Gray. Given how they'd parted that morning, she was both eager and wary. She wanted to be certain things were *right* between them, for lack of a better word. But the wariness... *That* came from something else. It came from her fear of wanting things she could not have.

There was nothing she had wanted more that morning than to have the freedom to say yes. And nothing had reminded her so clearly that the freedom she had found in London was an illusion built on fiction. Her entire identity was a lie. If she entered into a marriage under her assumed name, it would never be legal, and assuming they could even have children (something that, in her first marriage, had been cast into serious doubt), Gray would never have a legitimate heir. It was a house of cards destined to tumble. And if she were to out herself, to reveal the name she'd been given by birth, it was quite possible she'd be carted away to prison for murder.

Still, her breath quickened and her heart raced at the notion of another evening with him. Perhaps it was the fact that they always seemed to be on the verge of slipping away forever that made those evenings so precious.

"You're certain you have everything in hand?" she asked Bridget when the girl entered from the store-room, with Merilee behind her.

"Quite certain, ma'am," Bridget reassured her. "Merilee here is a treasure, and with the seamstresses now having extra help from my cousin, there's naught to keep you here tonight. I'll lock up and even come in extra early to open tomorrow."

"Bridget, do not ever underestimate your worth. You are a treasure as well," Sabine commented.

"Have a good evening, ma'am."

Sabine was gathering her things when she heard the girls' whispers. Her name was mentioned. Gray's was mentioned. Lovers was also overheard. But she didn't mind people knowing she was his lover. She was not some debutante entering the marriage market, after all. Virginity had no worth here in this world she'd thrust herself into by opening her little shop.

Exiting the shop via the back door that opened

into the alleyway, Sabine made for the street. But as she neared the end of the alleyway, placed purposefully on an upended crate, was a bouquet of white lilies. Her blood went cold at the sight. She detested those flowers. They were the only flowers Lawrence Russell had ever given her during their ridiculous sham of a courtship. They were the only ones he'd ever permitted in their home, either. Vase after vase in the entryway and on the dining table had been filled with them. Thee very scent of them now made her ill.

But it was the card nestled between the blooms which made her hands tremble. Reaching for it, though every instinct in her told her to leave it alone and run far away, she picked it up gingerly, almost as if it would bite her.

You have been missed.

—Your Bereaved Husband

LOGICALLY, there was every possibility that the flowers were not even intended for her. They might have been purchased by some truly grief-stricken husband who had second thoughts about taking himself to the cemetery. They were but a half mile from St. John's Church and the crypt there, and there were other small graveyards here and there along the way.

It was an unlikely scenario. But was it any less likely than the notion of her dead husband, murdered at her hand, not being dead at all and returning to bring her flowers she despised?

"He's dead," she whispered to herself. "The only thing haunting me are my own memories."

Is he? You never checked. You left him bleeding and ran as far and fast as you could. Mrs. Atkins could have lied to offer you peace of mind. It wouldn't be the first time.

That little niggle of doubt in the back of her mind left her feeling sick and weak. She hadn't checked. But surely no person could lose so much blood and survive? The floor had been covered with it. And if he had lived, if he had survived that desperate battle between them, then surely she would have heard before that moment? It would not have taken him four years to find her. He would have moved heaven and earth to bring her back, just to end her life on his terms. There was no question of it. He was not the sort to delay gratification or vengeance. Striking out at him that night, fighting back when, for years, she had been nothing but a cowering victim… That would have incited a rage in him like nothing else could. That she had wounded him so gravely. Indeed, had he survived, he would have come after her long before.

Speaking more firmly in an effort to convince herself, she said, "It can't possibly be. I'm overreacting out of fear. It's been an emotional day, and I'm seeing shadows of the past where they can't possibly exist."

With those words reverberating in her mind, Sabine walked ahead swiftly and purposely. She did not look behind her. No matter how urgently she wished to do so, she refused to give in to that desire. She dropped the cursed lilies and the cryptic note to the street and crushed them under her heel before continuing on. She would return home and dress for her evening excursion with Gray, and she would not allow thoughts of Lawrence Russell to rob her of a moment's pleasure.

▭

LAWRENCE FOLLOWED behind her at a safe distance. He'd watched her when she found the flowers. He'd noted the stark fear that showed on her face. He'd gloried in it as well. The woman who'd fought back like a tiger, who'd snatched a poker from the fireplace and nearly ended his life with it—that woman was an anomaly. She'd never been strong. She'd never had any fire within her. That was likely why she'd never been able to give him the son he required. She was pale, weak and insipid. Seeing her fear, seeing how she shivered and cowed when she'd read that note, had brought it all back for him.

"You'll pay, bitch," he muttered under his breath.

Beside him on the sidewalk, a woman gasped at his language. He didn't excuse himself or apologize. Instead, he turned to face the woman, his gaze cold and hard. Her eyes widened in fear, and she scurried along, another timid mouse afraid of her own shadow.

A frisson of excitement shot through him. He felt powerful. Making them shiver in terror, making them look over their shoulders or cower in fear, it had the blood pumping in his veins and his heart beating with anticipation. He could not wait to see her beg for her life. And he couldn't wait to choke it out of her while her eyes grew dim before him. The bitch would know, in the end, that she hadn't bested him.

Chapter Seven

Vauxhall Gardens had come alive as the sun had set. Dancers, mummers, acrobats and those performing astonishing feats of what could only be described as magic all careened wildly in that setting, forming a glittering and chaotic scene that was exciting and intoxicating all at once. It had the feeling of being in another world, and that was precisely why Gray had chosen it.

In Vauxhall, everyone wore masks. Demireps and duchesses sat side by side. Those masks were the great equalizer. It was a moment in time where Sabine would be his social equal, where she could hide her identity and finally be entirely herself. It was a calculated effort to get her to open up. One last valiant attempt, as it were, to get the information from her lips rather than through other clandestine sources.

Gray had obtained one of the more private boxes

for them. The curtains could be drawn, affording them complete privacy, or as much privacy as could be had in a crowd of thousands. The food had been ordered and already paid for, and it would be delivered as soon as Sabine arrived. Watching the growing crowd, he knew the moment she entered. He could see the silk cape fluttering behind her as she moved. It hadn't been worn for warmth but for effect. She moved like a goddess in it. Her hair was done up in a mass of curls, with some cascading over her neck in an imitation of amorous dishabille.

On her face, she wore the mask he'd had delivered to her home. The silver-and-gold domino, festooned with ostrich feathers and decorated with pearls, was a work of art, but certainly no more so than the woman who wore it.

"Good evening, sir," she said, as she neared the box.

"Good evening, madame," he replied. "I do not believe we have had the pleasure of an introduction. I am Edmund."

"Only Edmund? Surely a gentleman of your many charms should bear more than a simple moniker."

"On the contrary," he answered smoothly, "Tonight, I choose for things to be as simple as possible. We are two people sharing a meal together, in a somewhat private spot in a very public place. Our faces are well concealed. No one knows us. No one cares who we are. Tonight, in this box, we have the blessed gift of anonymity. So, I ask you, madame, what name shall I call you?"

She stared at him or a moment. Her hesitation was a palpable thing. Then her posture shifted, her chin lost that stubborn jut and, with no hint of her terrible accent, she replied, "You may call me Sally."

He didn't crow with victory, though the desire to do so was definitely present. It was an honest response from her. Of that, he was certain. Wherever she had been from, whomever she had been in the past, there wasn't a doubt in his mind that her name had been Sally. If he could cajole that much of the story from her, he could get more. And once he had the truth, then they could determine how best to proceed. "Join me, Sally," he invited, holding out his hand to her. "And let us see what pleasures these pleasure gardens can offer."

"What is this all about?" she asked, taking his hand as he helped her into the box. "You won't change my answer from this morning."

"I'm not trying to change your answer. But I would like to understand it. For that, I thought meeting on neutral ground, with a bit of armor"—he reached out to touch her face, his thumb tracing the edge of her mask—"might help."

She didn't say anything in reply, as the waiter, true to his word, had appeared with food the moment she had arrived. All the items were deposited on their table, including the infamous wafer-thin slices of ham. Once their repast had been carefully placed on the small table, the waiter backed out of the box, with a bow.

Alone, Gray rose from his seat and drew the gauzy curtains together until they were almost entirely closed. Someone would need to walk to the very edge of their box to see them, though they could still see out. "Now, we should not be interrupted for some time to come."

"I suppose, under the circumstances, you are entitled to some explanation," she mused, even as she reached for the freshly opened bottle of wine and began to pour it into the glasses that had been provided.

"I should like one," Gray said, then added, "I do not know that anyone is entitled to it. I want you to tell me so that I may help you to face whatever is or to resolve it. Not because you owe it to me."

"You cannot resolve this," she said grimly. "I murdered my husband."

It was not really what he'd expected her to say, at least not so boldly. "Murdered or killed? That's an important distinction."

A sad smile tugged at her lips, and her gaze held an expression of weariness that hinted at how long she had truly been suffering. "He is dead either way, and the law would hold me accountable for it if it were known," she replied.

Gray sipped his wine and then leaned back on the banquette. "Tell me what happened."

"He was a violent man. Cold and very cruel. And I was so terribly young when I married him. The entire thing was arranged by my father. He owed a debt to him, you see, so at sixteen years old, I was paraded to the church and given to a monster in lieu of payment. I should be thankful, I suppose, that it was for the sake of marriage rather than to simply to be used and discarded."

"Except that, then, you would have been free to walk away of your own accord," Gray stated.

She glanced up at him in surprise, her dark eyes perfectly framed by the domino she wore. "Well, yes. I had never really considered that. Freedom of any sort is something women are not generally permitted to think of. We go from being the property of our fathers to being the property of our husbands. I had to assume a false identity as a widowed Frenchwoman in order to have any sort of autonomy in my own life," she remarked.

"And the night he died?"

"The night I killed him," she corrected. "If we're going to speak of it, let us speak bluntly. He was furious because I had not presented him with a son, or even a child at all. We had been married for four years at that point. Four years of torment and terror. Four long and horrid years of enduring his touch, ham-fisted at best and intentionally cruel at worst…

And in spite of how wretched it was, I prayed that I would never become with child. Because I couldn't bear the thought of that child living under the same roof with the monster that would have been its father."

Gray didn't interject, nor did he ask the hundreds of questions that seemed to be whirling through his mind. It was her story to tell, after all, not an inquisition.

After a moment, she continued, "At any rate, that prayer was answered. It seemed as though it would never happen. I suppose he certainly thought so. I'd taken his beatings and his belittlement; I no longer cared about that. I knew if he beat me senseless there would be a reprieve, you see? For a few weeks, at least, things would be normal. Not good or bad, really, but just normal. But that night was different. He said I was defective or damaged. That my father likely knew I was a broken excuse for a woman when he passed me off to him. If I hadn't given him an heir by then, I never would. So what good was I?" She stopped then, her gaze far away and a muscle ticking in her jaw as she revisited those terrible memories.

Again, he didn't interrupt, nor did he feel the need to prod her. She would tell it in her own time and in her own way—and at her own cost. It was a terrible thing to realize that his demand for answers had caused her pain, that she was reliving the nightmare of her past for his benefit.

"I knew that it was different," she began again, her voice much softer. "He wasn't enraged, not at all. He was quite calm. A bottle of laudanum was in his pocket. He took it out and poured the entire contents of it into a glass, set it in front of me, and told me I could drink it of my own accord, else he'd force it down my throat."

Gray's fists clenched tightly, but he didn't move. He didn't shout with anger or disbelief, though the callousness she described was difficult to imagine. "And how did you respond?"

"I laughed at first," she said. "I thought it couldn't possibly… How could anyone expect that a person would do such a thing? Even as miserable as I was, I'd survived by thinking that, at his age, I would certainly outlive him. That I would eventually be a widow and free of him. I had never entertained the thought of ending my own life… That's when his rage came. When I dared to laugh and to disobey him, that's when the monster I knew suddenly reappeared. He grabbed my hair and forced me onto the floor, on my knees. He struck me. He slapped me with such force that I think only fear kept me from losing conscious-ness. But when I fell backward from the force of the blow, my hand hit the tiles before the fireplace. And I scrambled backward instinctively until I could reach the poker."

She raised the glass to her lips and drank deeply. In one long gulp, she had consumed almost the entire glass of wine before placing it once more on the table. It bobbled slightly in her trembling hands.

Gray lifted the bottle and refilled it immediately. She might be speaking matter-of-factly, but the tension in her, the haunted look in her eyes, told the truth of it. Every second of the ordeal was being re-lived by her. Every emotion, every second of dread, was as real to her in that moment as if it was happening all over again.

"It isn't any great stretch of the imagination to deduce what happened after. He came at me, and I picked up the poker and swung it at him. I caught him on the side of his head, here." She lifted one finger to her temple. "He fell to the floor, but he was still moving. So, I hit him again. And then he didn't move. Even his breathing seemed to have stopped. I took the money from his pocket, and that which was hidden in his bedchamber, along with all the jewelry that I could quickly lay hands on, and I ran. No clothes, no bags, no time to even formulate an idea of where I would go… Nothing. It was all instinct, like a fox going to ground when the hounds are chasing it. I took the stage to Bath first, then again to Birmingham. From there, I hired a coach to take me to Edinburgh. Then I booked passage and sailed back to Brighton and made my way here. I hoped that taking a circuitous route would help me to stay well ahead of him."

"It certainly couldn't have helped. But you said he was dead, so why run?"

"I thought him so. I kept watching the papers, searching for any mention of it. I never found one. There was so much blood. He couldn't have survived."

Gray wasn't so certain. "Head wounds bleed like the devil, Sabine—Sally. They are very deceptive in that way. If you tell me his name, I will find out if he lives."

"No. Because whether he is alive or whether he is dead, it changes nothing. If he lives, I cannot marry you because I am already married to another. If he is dead, I cannot marry you because I will not risk embarrassing you publicly by being carted out of our home to the gaol for being a murderess. Can't you see that what we have is a gift? To dare ask for more—to expect more—would be the height of foolishness."

"What I can see is that you call this freedom when it is not. You've only added a few more links to the chains that bind you," he replied.

Chapter Eight

Sabine sighed. It was so much simpler when ntheir hearts weren't involved. When it had all just been heat and desire and no thoughts of a future together, it had been easy. Now, she wanted things she shouldn't. She certainly wanted things she could not have. And so did he. "Sally is gone. She is dead, whether her husband is or not. The woman who sits before you today is Sabine. I am who I have chosen to be. I have an income that suits me. Thanks to you, I have a home that is far grander than anything I have ever known. But I will not be bullied into marrying you. Nor will I be pushed into confronting the past when nothing good can come of it. Poking at a hornet's nest will only get one stung. I've suffered enough already. If you cannot accept this…if you cannot accept me as I am, then you must tell me now."

"Do not," he replied.

"Do not what?"

"Do not make this about ultimatums and power. That is not the reason behind it, and you know it! I can see your fear, Sabine. I can feel it when I touch you," he stated. "I want to see you safe and secure. Given a chance, I would like to provide that security. But, whatever happens between us, I would not see this hanging over your head indefinitely. Let me help you."

"No," she stated emphatically. God, but she loved him. She loved that he wanted to be her savior, to rescue her from all the things that could make her life hard or dangerous. But not even he had the ability to unmake her past, much as he might believe otherwise. If—and it was a very great if—Lawrence was not dead, there was no power on Earth that could save her from him. "There is no help for it. It is a situation where it is simply best to let sleeping dogs lie. You can either accept that, and we can continue as we have been, or I can go home…alone."

"And that sounds suspiciously like an ultimatum, Sabine."

"It is. I've built a life here. If you draw attention to me by attempting to dig up my past, it places that life in jeopardy, both literally and figuratively. I've run once. I do not want to have to do so again, not from you. Please, Gray. I'm begging you to let this alone. I can't marry you, but it doesn't mean I want to give you up. I do not. I'd give anything if we could just go back to last night, to the way things were. Can't we?"

"You aren't giving me any other choice," he answered. "I can't let you go. No matter that my pride will demand it at some point. For now, I can't bear to think of it. So, the subject will be dropped. Your past and our future are off the table for the moment. We shall focus only on the present. The here and now."

Sabine picked up her wine glass and raised it in a toast. "To us. To here and now." It would be enough, she determined. It would have to be.

Their conversation halted then as a group of performers ambled by. There were jugglers and acrobats and dancers, all darting to and fro while carrying torches and lanterns. It made a dazzling display that, at least momentarily, relieved some of the tension that had gathered between them. Focusing on those sights, Sabine's lips quirked at their antics. All the while, she could feel Gray watching her, could feel his speculation. He was a protector, naturally. It was simply who he was. He took his responsibilities very seriously, and for better or worse, because he cared for her, he saw her as that—as his responsibility. She loved him for it almost as much as she resented that intrusion on her carefully crafted illusion of freedom. After what she'd endured at the hands of Lawrence Russell, it was difficult to cede so much of her power to any man, even one whom she trusted.

At that moment, one of the performers paused in

front of their box. Painted in harlequin makeup and garbed in a worn silk costume, the man grinned maniacally at them before proceeding to blow some sort of liquid from his mouth onto the torch he held. Flames shot upward into the night sky. Sabine let out a startled shriek, followed by nervous laughter. It was terrifying and exciting all at once. Then the man produced a single flower from up his sleeve and dropped it at her feet before gamboling away.

Stooping to pick up the flower, Sabine's heart stuttered in her chest. A sick feeling of dread settled in the pit of her stomach as she looked at the lily. There was a small card attached to the flower with a bit of thin ribbon.

You are missed.

Not *have been*. Not *were*. Nothing in it reflected that it was past. It was all very much present. Here and now, Gray had said. It seemed that they were not even to have that.

GRAY WATCHED HER, noting the exact moment when her expression shifted from one of somewhat startled amusement to something else. He could see her fear. Terror rolled off her in waves, like water cascading over rocks.

"What is it, Sabine?"

"We need to go. Now," she said. "We must leave immediately. We are too exposed here."

"What does that flower mean to you? What does it signify?"

"It means that the past I tried to run away from has caught up to me at last. It means that you do not have to worry about digging it up. It is here now, and I will have to pay for what I have done."

"Your husband? The man you thought you had killed… You think he is here?" Gray demanded. "It's only a flower."

She passed the flower to him, the small card dangling from the delicate ribbon. He read it. "It could be nothing."

"I found another one earlier today. An entire bouquet of them. It said, 'You have been missed,' and was signed, 'your bereaved husband.' They were his favorite, you know. He filled the house with them. So much so that it perpetually smelled like we were hosting a wake," she explained. "Once I could call coincidence. But twice in a matter of hours? No, Gray. He's here. He's here, and he wants me to know it. And—"

He waited for her to continue but when she said nothing further, he pressed, "And what?"

"I thought I saw him. This morning as I walked to the shop, I glanced over my shoulder, and I thought I saw him standing there. But I tripped and fell, and when I looked back, he was gone."

He didn't argue the point. There was still every possibility that it was not him but someone else from their past. But it certainly bore investigating. And he would not leave her to her fears. The memory of the man he'd seen lurking in the mews filtered to the surface. Could it have been him? "You will stay with me."

"I cannot possibly! The scandal would ruin you. I have to go."

"Where?" he demanded. "If you cannot get lost in the anonymity of a city the size of London, then you cannot truly be lost anywhere. Let me help you, Sabine. Scandal be damned."

"You've done so much already! It will ruin you."

"I will be ruined, perhaps. But is ruination in the eyes of society any worse than the wreckage that will be left of me if I let you go? If something happens to you?" he asked. "No, Sabine. They can gossip as they like. Wag their tongues until they fall straight out of their mouths. I do not care. But if you are in danger, I will keep you safe, whatever the cost. Come. We'll go now."

He could see her indecision. The war she fought within herself was clearly marked in the turbulence so evident in her gaze. After a long and torturous moment, she raised her hand and placed it in his.

"I cannot let you do something so damaging, but I will compromise. You will stay in my home. It's a different thing altogether for a man to pass weeks in a home he provides for his mistress. It's another altogether to waltz her into his family home as if she's the right to it."

"You do have the right to it," he insisted.

"Only in your eyes.

"My only regret in this life is that I did not meet you before this bastard staked his claim," Gray responded honestly. "I'd have married you then and spared you all that he put you through and all the time we've lost because of it."

Hand in hand, they exited Vauxhall and made their way to his carriage, parked near the gates. Servants would be instructed to gather her things. Instructions would be sent to her shop. And for the foreseeable future, he would not let her out of his sight.

▭

LAWRENCE RUSSELL WATCHED his wife as she left the private box with her lover. Fury washed through him at the sight of them. He didn't want her. He never wanted the bitch again, but it galled that she'd be out living the high life with another man after she'd bludgeoned him and left him for dead. *Faithless whore.*

Following through the throng of revelers, he never let the couple from his sight. Weaving between the chaotic dancers and attendees, he watched as they exited through the main gate and climbed into a carriage bedecked with his coat of arms.

"Grasping bitch," he spat. She'd set her sights high all right. It had been in her eyes when she'd looked at him, even when he'd courted her. She'd wanted someone younger, handsomer, richer, titled.

It wasn't really a conscious thing, deciding to kill her lover, the Earl of Winburn. But as he watched the couple make their escape, his resentment grew. It became a ravening beast trapped inside him. Clawing and hungry, it demanded blood. And hers would not be enough to appease it.

Yes, indeed. The soon-to-be-discarded mistress would kill her lover, slitting his throat as he slept, rather than see him leave her for another. Then, overcome with grief at what she'd done, she'd down a whole bottle of laudanum to join him in his eternal slumber. He might not kill her with his bare hands as he first intended, but watching her shriek in agony at the sight of her murdered lover would do just as well.

Lawrence grinned, a wicked-looking expression as it pulled the scar at his hairline, turning it stark white against his skin. He looked very much what he was in that moment—a madman.

Chapter Nine

They retreated to her smaller home. Sabine led him up the stairs to her chamber. Her decision was made, and he would hate her for it, but she knew that to save them both, there was only one option: She would have to flee. Once more, Lawrence Russell was robbing her of everything that was wonderful and joyful in her life. But not immediately. She would take these last hours with Gray and make them a memory to comfort them both.

As they entered her bedchamber, Sabine released the ties holding the elaborate domino in place and laid it on the table. Her fingers trailed over the intricate embellishments of the silk. "It was a beautiful night you created for us…and my past has overshadowed it."

"That is not your fault. Knowing you better, knowing your hopes and fears, those things make me close to you in a way that I have not been before," he said softly. "Unpleasant though those memories are, I'm glad you shared them with me."

Sabine glanced over her shoulder at him, a smile curving her lips. "You truly are the best of men. I do not think that you appreciate what a rarity that is. If I live a hundred years, I shall never know anyone else quite like you."

"Then live a hundred years. Live them at my side. I shall strive for less perfection so that you won't get bored," he teased.

"I shall never be bored in your presence, my lord," she stated, strolling over to where he stood. She reached up and lifted the domino from his face, setting it aside with her own. Then she reached for his cravat, her fingers moving nimbly over the intricate knot until the fabric slipped free. "Indeed, my own thoughts in your presence put me to blush."

"You will not distract me so easily from our previous conversation," he stated. "We need to determine the best course to keep you safe."

Sabine slipped her hand beneath his coat, easing the well-fitted garment from his broad shoulders. "Naught can be done about that until the morning. Correct?"

He sighed heavily. But there was a note of resignation in it. "I suppose that is true enough."

She pushed the coat off him completely, before draping it over the chair. Without hesitation, she began working the buttons of his waistcoat free. "It stands to reason that the best way to see to my safety would be to stay close to my side. Proximity is a necessity, I would dare say."

When his waistcoat joined his other garments, she slipped her hands beneath his shirt, feeling the warmth and firmness of his skin. She scraped lightly with her nails over his back, and his breath hissed out.

"You are playing with fire," he warned.

"Then, burn with me." She didn't wait for a response. Instead, she shifted her hand to the fall of his breeches. The rigid length of him was immediately evident as she stroked him through the fabric. Within seconds, he'd swooped her into his arms and carried her back to the bed.

She wasn't even certain how it happened, but her clothing simply fell away. They were naked, their bodies twined together as he kissed her hungrily. Sabine clung to him, savoring the heat and the strength of him, committing it to memory, even as the familiar swell of desire rose inside her. Even after more than a year with him, the swiftness of her response, the intensity of it, was always a shock.

He played her body like an instrument, knowing precisely where and how to touch her, how to escalate the mounting tension inside her to a fever pitch. When she could do nothing more than cry out brokenly at the intense need that he had created, only then did he offer her relief. He slipped his hand between her thighs, pressing against her as his fingers stroked her most tender flesh. God, he could make her burn in ways she had never imagined. In his arms, she became like a wild thing, needful and demanding.

When he captured her hands in one of his, he brought them up and pinned them above her head. But she didn't panic; she never did with him. With him, she always felt safe. He needed to feel in control, and she, in that moment, needed to pretend that he was. It was a balm for them both.

"Tell me," he urged.

"I want you," she whispered.

"Not that. That, I know. Tell me what I need to hear from you, Sabine."

He was asking her to make herself vulnerable to him, to say words that would bind them forever. But they were bound regardless of whether those words were spoken or not. "I love you. I will always love you."

Then he was sinking into her, parting her flesh and staking a claim that would never be broken. They could be thousands of miles apart, and she would be no less his than she was in that moment.

As always, when their passions rose, when the pleasure became this omnipresent thing that consumed them, thought simply fled. She gave in to the sensations and allowed them to simply sweep her into that abyss. He soon followed.

In the aftermath, the room was quiet, save for the

sound of their ragged breathing. Sabine lay there, waiting for sleep to claim him. As the sound of his breath evened, as the tension in his body began to seep away, she did the thing that was so much harder than she might have ever imagined. She eased from beneath the weight of his arm and rose from the bed. Sparing one last glance back at him, she retrieved her wrapper from the foot of the bed and slipped silently from the room.

It had been laundry day. Making for the small room off the kitchen where the items had been placed to dry, she donned fresh stockings, a chemise, petticoat, stays, and then a simple woolen gown. There were a pair of sturdy boots there as well, having recently been given a good polish. There was a cloak, too, lightweight but needed for rain. It was also a dingy enough garment that no one would think her a lady if she wore it. It was the perfect disguise. The invisibility of the lower class.

Fully dressed, she stuffed the other items that were there into a small valise that had been tucked into a cupboard under the stairs. From the small room she used as an office, she retrieved the funds she'd been storing away in case she ever needed to make an escape.

At the door, she paused. Her hand hovered over the door handle for the longest time. God, she didn't want to leave him behind. Not him. Not the life she had made for herself. But it would ruin him if the truth about her came out, because he was too good to walk away from her even to save himself.

After a deep, shuddering breath, she opened that door and stepped out into the darkness. It was well after midnight. Hailing a hack, she instructed the driver to take her to The Golden Cross Inn. She'd depart for the last place in the world that Lawrence Russell would think to look for her. She was going home.

<hr>

GRAY WASN'T ENTIRELY certain what had awoken him. But as he rolled over in the bed, he knew that he was alone. He also knew that he had been for some time. Sabine was gone. Getting up, he dressed as quickly as possible. He didn't bother to check to see if she'd taken anything with her. He knew that she would have. She'd been planning it from the moment they'd left Vauxhall, no doubt.

"Damn her," he cursed. "Damn her to hell."

Forcing himself to think, he made several decisive deductions. At the time of night she had fled, there would be only a number of places she could have gone. And if she wanted to vacate the city, it narrowed them even further. Coaching inns, and particularly those from whence the mail coaches departed, would be her most likely starting point.

A young boy ran by just then. He was dousing the

streetlamp. "Boy, which of the inns in London are mail coach departures?"

"Well, sir, there be but four. The closest one is at Charring Cross. The Golden Cross, it be."

"And do you know what time the mail coach leaves there?"

"Two hours past, sir," the boy said.

Gray tossed him a coin. "Thank you."

He didn't make for the Golden Cross. It was too late. Instead, he made for home. He'd never catch her by carriage. He'd need to go on horseback. To that end, he made for home.

Chapter Ten

By the time the mail coach reached Northampton, Sabine had been beset with second thoughts. Now, halfway between Northampton and Nottingham, she was having third, fourth, or possibly twentieth thoughts. Allowing that most of her doubts were born out of discomfort, there was still a not-insignificant portion that was born of something else altogether.

It would have hurt him when he discovered her gone. No doubt he would see it as some sort of lack of faith in his ability to protect her. And it wasn't. She'd known that he would, without question. But there would be a price for him to pay for that protection, and she couldn't bear to be the cause of his regret. He wouldn't understand a man like Lawrence Russell. For Gray, honor wasn't just a trait he possessed. It was in the very fabric of his being. Gray would protect her at any cost, but that cost would alter him forever, and that was something she could not live with. It seemed, when it came to him, that she had her own brand of honor.

The driver began ringing the bell, indicating that they would change horses at the next coaching inn. It wasn't much of a break on the long journey, but it was the only opportunity she'd have to stretch her legs. Many of her fellow travelers would partake of food at the inn, prepared to be eaten quickly and often on the go. For herself, she couldn't stand the thought of food. The weight of her decision was pressing on her so much that it would likely make her ill if she did eat.

When the mail coach rattled into the inn yard, she was eager to disembark and ease the many aches and pains that such prolonged sitting and terrible jostling had caused. Eight hours on the road, and there were still another twelve to go before they reached Doncaster.

When the coach doors opened, her fellow travelers stepped down, one by one. Sabine was the last one out of the coach. She gratefully accepted the hand to aid her down, thinking it would be one of her fellow travelers, an ostler, or even one of the guards. But the holt of recognition she felt at that touch halted her in her tracks, so much so that she very nearly stumbled down the remaining step.

"Hello, Sabine."

"Gray," she said breathlessly, "what are you doing here?"

"Running you to ground, it would seem," he stated, with no small amount of irritation. "You lied to me."

"I never said I would stay."

"You never said you would leave, either," he pointed out. "A lie by omission is still a lie. And I won't have those between us. Never again. Come inside. I've obtained a private parlor for us and their best room. The innkeeper thinks I am here to meet my wife after a long absence from her."

"Now who is the liar?" she demanded.

"Would you have me tell him the truth? That you are on the run from both your nearly-late husband and your lover? If one wishes to travel unobtrusively, that is hardly the way," he answered drolly.

"You're angry. You are always flippant when you are angry."

"You're damn right I'm angry," he said, his eyes flashing with temper as he cut them toward her. "What if he'd been watching the house? What if he'd seen you leave? What if *he'd* followed that coach and had been lying in wait for you along this road, instead of me?"

She'd thought of it. She understood that there were risks involved in her plan, but they were calculated risks. Lawrence wouldn't act so quickly. He enjoyed playing cat and mouse too much for that. "I was safe enough."

"Clearly, you are too insensible to accurately gauge such a thing," he snapped.

Sabine didn't protest. He was in no mood to hear her reasons. Instead, she allowed him to lead her into the inn and to the small private parlor that he had obtained for them. The room was stuffy, the dark wood and heavy fabric at the windows limiting any chance of a breeze entering the room, though the windows were open. A small meal had been laid for them, consisting mostly of cold meats and bread. There were jugs of ale or wine (which, she could not be certain). Gray closed the door behind them, muffling the noisy taproom.

"I'll need my bag from the mail coach," she said.

"It's taken care of," he stated flatly, and made a sweeping gesture toward a darkened corner of the room.

Sabine's gaze landed on the worn valise. "You were very certain that I would remain with you."

"I hadn't really planned to give you a choice in the matter," he answered.

"You're abducting me?"

"If need be," he said. "I'd like to think you will be reasonable enough that abduction will not be necessary."

He said it with no care at all for the degree of his autocracy. Sabine's eyebrows raised, and a smile curved her lips, but it was not an expression that really hinted at amusement. "You seem to be laboring under the misapprehension that I will tolerate your high-handedness, Gray. I will not. I do not need you to rescue me. I was doing just fine all on my own."

"I never said you weren't. Perhaps I'm not here because you need to be rescued, Sabine. Perhaps I'm here because I simply cannot fathom how to continue my life when you would not be in it," he answered. "I think it is less a matter of abduction than it is of joining you as you run away."

"Uninvited."

He shrugged. "Do I require an invitation? But perhaps you were not running from your late husband so much as the man who wishes to be your future husband."

She might have dismissed it, that offhand remark. But there was a note in his voice, a tightness there, that hinted at his pain. She had hurt him, but not at all in the way she imagined.

"If I were free to marry, I'd never have paused before shouting my acceptance to the very stars," she said softly. "But I am not free, and wishing it were otherwise will not make it so. He will hunt me down. And if you try to protect me, he will not hesitate to see you removed from his path. This isn't the sort of thing that can be fixed with a gentleman's agreement or even a duel. He'd be more likely to hire a footpad to stick a knife in your ribs as you walk the streets of Mayfair. You do not understand him, Gray. Not the way I do."

"Then make me understand him. Stop hiding the facts of it from me as if I were some sheltered child," he snapped.

Sabine sighed wearily. "Now that you've caught me, what is your plan?"

"Well, clearly you mean to make for your home, do you not? I cannot imagine you would have taken this particular coach otherwise."

"I had," she stated. "Though I was uncertain about whether or not I would remain there. I thought it would be the least likely route of pursuit he would take."

"I have a small villa at Boston Spa. I thought we might go there. It is close enough to York that we may make inquiries about him in a reasonable manner," he said.

"What sort of inquiries? I know all of him that I require!"

GRAY STARED at her for a moment. How could he so desperately want to hold her close and shake some sense into her all at once? "He's a brutal man. You've never told me the particulars of his brutality, but I've seen the evidence of it clearly enough, haven't I?"

She looked away. "I do not wish to discuss that."

"Then, do not. I'll discuss it." Leaning across the table, he tore a hunk of bread from the loaf that had been placed there. "Brutal men do brutal things, Sabine. If you think you are the only person to suffer at his hands, then you are blind. Men like him, they will have left a trail of misery and discontent in their wake. We only need to follow his trail of destruction."

"Most people who have dealt with him will be too fearful to speak of it," she insisted.

"I am an earl. I have the ability to offer them protection—and a not insignificant sum for their troubles," he replied. "We will find what we need to bring him to heel."

"And, yet, I will still be his wife."

"Not when they hang him," Gray answered. "And I mean to see to it that they will. He deserves nothing less than that for what he forced you to endure. You are so focused on what he is capable of, Sabine, that you have not considered at all what I am capable of. Perhaps you should."

Chapter Eleven

It wasn't the first time she'd been in one of Gray's homes. It was, however, the first time she'd entered it as a guest rather than clandestinely and under the cover of darkness. On the surface, everything appeared fine. But Sabine was not so foolish that she did not recognize the coldness of the butler or the way that the housekeeper would not look directly at her. The villa in Boston Spa was not so grand as his London abode, but the servants were clearly just as discriminating. She understood her place in the world, but he did not. Gray saw only what was right before him, what he wished to see. His single-mindedness, in many regards, was an asset. But she had her doubts about its benefit in their current arena.

"Madame de Roussard will be staying for the foreseeable future," he instructed the housekeeper. "Tomorrow, at first light, you will send servants to her home on Carpenter Street to collect anything she might require during her stay. In the interim, provide her with anything that is necessary. No doubt my sister has left enough items behind during her visits to my grandmother that our guest's comfort can be seen to without any great difficulty. Also, have tea delivered to the study. Madame de Roussard and I have much to discuss, given the particulars of her stay here."

Sabine watched the servants bow, scrape, and scurry at his orders. There were not many of them, given that the house had been closed up, but they were great enough in number that gossip would flow freely. She could already feel their resentment. Following Gray to his study, she stepped inside and seated herself in one of heavily upholstered chairs there. It was a masculine room, rich and dark, in earthy shades of leather and velvet. There was a hint of tobacco in the air, but also a musty smell indicating he had not been there to use that room for some time.

"They will hate me," she said softly. "They have already taken my measure and found me wanting. They are likely whispering, even now, that you have brought your whore with you."

His head came up, and his expression was dark. "I have never thought of you that way."

"You do not have to, Gray. That is how others see me. It is the reality of our station and our arrangement. The finer feelings we may possess for one another aside, you've brought a disreputable woman into your house, and you expect your servants to treat her as an exalted guest. And they will, because they value their employment, but they will hate me for it."

He was silent and stony for a moment. Then he simply shrugged. "Then, I shall hire new servants, if necessary. You will not be treated poorly here, or it will be dealt with. As to their hatred, they may feel it all they like so long as they do not show it. I call it a small price to maintain your safety, don't you?"

In those terms, yes, she thought. "I've been hated before. No doubt, I shall survive it."

"What is his name?" Gray demanded in a soft voice. "This husband who is both dead and undead simultaneously. You've never said, and if I am to discover his darkest secrets, I will need to know it."

"Lawrence Russell," she answered. At this point, if he did live, there was no need to conceal his name. "He owns several mills in Yorkshire. He has no title and no connections to the peerage, but he was well respected there and had the ear of many. He can wreak havoc if he chooses."

"He will not. I will see to it. If I have to challenge the bloody bastard to a duel and end his miserable life myself, I will do so."

"And live in exile?" she all but shrieked. "No. I will not let you sacrifice your life that way."

"I'm a very good shot."

She shook her head. "You are being deliberately obtuse. You'd have to leave England, live in exile...

Everything you love would be sacrificed! Your title, your home, your family!"

"Not everything," he said softly. "Not everything, Sabine… Sally."

It felt so strange to hear that name, to respond to it as if it were once again her own. He'd taken that from her, she realized. Lawrence Russell had robbed her of her joy, her innocence, and her identity. "Sabine," she corrected, "I'm not sure Sally exists anymore. Even if she does, I like who I am now much better. But if that girl does exist, somewhere in the darkest depths of my soul, you are the only one who might be able to discover her."

"You know what I feel for you. You must."

Her heart did a strange fluttering thing in her chest. She pressed her hand there, between her breasts, trying to still it even as she struggled to draw breath. "Do not say things you will regret," she cautioned.

"I've no regrets. I love you. Were you free, I would marry you tomorrow. I would marry you in this very moment. And I need a promise from you, Sally Lawrence, that when this is all settled and done, you will be mine—not out of gratitude or necessity, but because you wish to be."

There was a vulnerability in him that surprised her. She'd glimpsed it from time to time over the course of their relationship, but it was much closer to the surface in that moment, shimmering beneath his facade of confidence. So, she gave him a far more honest answer than she had ever intended to. "Whatever occurs, I am already yours. I always have been."

Gray stared at her for a moment longer, then gave a nod, almost as if he didn't trust himself to speak. Finally, clearing his throat a bit, he offered, "I'll have one of the maids show you to your chamber. I will join you there after the household is abed. I must speak with the butler about setting up patrols on the grounds, especially by the garden gates."

Sabine felt a frisson of fear at that statement. "I couldn't bear it if something happened to you because of me."

"Nothing will happen to me," he assured her. "And nothing will happen to you. This is a fight he cannot win; I promise you that."

Sabine wished she could have his confidence in the matter. But Lawrence Russell was the sum of all evil for her. When things went bump in the night, it wasn't ghouls or goblins she feared but him. "I am suddenly very tired." The exhaustion of days of worry, or fleeing London in the night, of traveling at such a brutal pace—it had all suddenly caught up with her.

"Should I not come to you later?"

"If you can, you should. I always sleep better when you are beside me," she admitted. It was because he made her feel safe and protected. But that was an easier thing to do before she understood that Lawrence knew precisely where to find her.

———

GRAY WATCHED as she rose and exited the study. A maid was waiting for her at the door to show her to her chamber. He'd had her placed near him. Not so near that it would raise eyebrows, but near enough that he wouldn't have to traipse naked through the entire house to reach her. Of course, it was a small house. That would help tremendously.

No sooner had she departed than the butler entered the study. Gray noted the man's disapproving frown but elected to ignore it. Instead, he focused on the more prevailing matter at hand. "Devers, I have every reason to believe that Madame de Roussard is in danger. There is someone who poses a significant threat to her, and I have placed her under this roof that she might be protected. Your personal feelings about my relationship with her aside, can you see to it that the footmen or stable lads are making adequate patrols about the house and gardens, to ensure that there will be no uninvited guests trying to enter the property?"

The butler cleared his throat. "I am in service to you, my lord. I have no opinions that you have not given me leave to do so. I will be certain that the house and grounds are locked up as tightly as possible, and there will be footmen stationed at every entrance and exit to prevent any threats from reaching the… er…lady."

"That'll do well enough, then, Devers. Thank you."

"Do you require anything else, my lord?"

"No, Devers. That will be all. I bid you goodnight. I will see to some matters here before going to bed. Other than the footman at the entrances, the other servants may retire, as well. The house will be in uproar enough tomorrow." And it would. It was one thing to set up a mistress in another house acquired for that purpose. It was quite another to set her up in one's own home, even if it was not his primary residence. People would talk. Her presence there would not go unnoticed for long.

Her words echoed in his mind, that Sally, the girl she had once been, was gone forever. When the issue of Lawrence Russell was resolved once and for all, he intended to prove her wrong on that score. He intended to help her rediscover herself, to find some sort of joy in life, rather than simply living moment to moment in fear.

Chapter Twelve

Sabine awoke still somewhat groggy. The bed beside her was empty, but she could still see the imprint on the pillow where Gray had slept beside her during the night. They hadn't made love. She'd been asleep when he entered her room, and he'd simply removed his clothing, lain down beside her, and wrapped her in his arms. They'd slept like that through the whole of the night. At some point, just before dawn, he'd arisen and made his way back to his own chambers.

Of course, she was well aware that they were not fooling anyone. She was both more and less than his house guest, and as the maid moved about the room, lighting the fire and tidying up, it was obvious that she knew it as well. The girl would not even raise her head for fear of having to make eye contact with a fallen woman.

"What is your name?" Sabine asked.

The girl halted, like a deer or rabbit when it sensed a predator was nearby. "Alice, ma'am," the girl muttered.

"Alice, I do not bite. I know I am not welcome here. I know that the servants think I am too far beneath his lordship to be catered to by anyone. If I had any choice in the matter, I would not be here. I would remain in my own home and in my own place. Be sure to let them all know that. I have no intentions of trying to play lady of the house."

Alice nodded again. "Yes, ma'am. I'll be certain to let them all know. Good day, ma'am. Another maid will be in to help you dress."

With the girl scurrying down the hall, her face no doubt beet redb, Sabine stretched and rose. She walked from the bed over to the window that looked down on the garden below. There was a footman positioned at the garden gate. Near the small stable at the back, there was a much rougher looking man. She had little doubt there would be sentries posted at every door, just the same. Gray was a man of his word, after all, and he would move heaven and earth to keep her safe.

At that moment, another maid entered. This one didn't have the same meekness as Alice. Her shoulders were straight, her chin was up, and it was quite obvious from the set of her jaw that she was appalled at having to cater to a woman who was little better than a doxy.

"What is your name?" Sabine asked her.

"Betsy, Madame de Roussard. I acted as lady's maid to his lordship's sister when she would come to visit the dowager."

"I see, Betsy. Thank you for your assistance this morning. I assume you've sorted out the mess that was in my valise?"

"Yes, ma'am. I've got a dress pressed and waiting in the dressing room beyond. Would you care for a bath now, or will you break your fast first and have it later in the afternoon?"

"Now, I think. I couldn't eat a bite," Sabine answered her.

"Very well, ma'am. I'll see to it," Betsy said, and promptly turned on her heel to depart.

Within a quarter hour, a copper tub in the dressing room had been filled with warm water. Entering that much smaller chamber, Betsy was awaiting her there. Sabine simply removed her wrapper and chemise and stepped into the tub. She heard the maid's gasp. There was no hiding her scars, and she didn't intend to try. It was a futile exercise.

"What in the world happened?" the maid exclaimed.

"A man, of course," Sabine answered. "What always happens to women?"

The maid said nothing more. She saw to the bath, helped Sabine wash her hair, and then combed it rigorously. With those tasks completed, Sabine was seated before the fire to let her hair dry. It would take ages, but she didn't regret the decision not to take herself down to breakfast. The fewer prying eyes and whispers she had to face, the better.

"Will be there anything else until we can dress your hair, ma'am?"

"No, Betsy, that will be all."

"I'll see to unpacking and pressing the rest of your things," the maid answered. But as she reached the door, the girl paused. "I seen scars like that before, ma'am. I know what they come from. My brother was a sailor and was flogged aboard ship."

Sabine stiffened, but said nothing. "I have a great deal of sympathy for him, then."

"It wasn't his lordship what did that to you. He's not the sort."

"No, he isn't," Sabine agreed. "He's not like anyone else."

Betsy did look at her then, glancing back over her shoulder. "I know what folks has been saying below stairs… You showing up here with him, bold as brass and no chaperone in sight. I know they talk and whisper about everyone's business but their own. You're not what I thought you'd be."

"And what is that, Betsy?"

"Cold and hard. A woman out for what she could get. But you're not with him for what he gives you, are you? It's not about houses and jewels for you, at all."

"No, Betsy, I'm not in it for those things, but I've

no illusions about how all of this ends. I'm not for him, ultimately. No matter what he might think."

The maid cocked her head to one side. "Life has a way of surprising us, ma'am. I've been in this house since I was a girl, taking care of the dowager and watching how he took care of her when she was at the end. He's an honorable man, but I've never known his lordship not to have his way, no matter it is. He won't push, he won't bully. But he'll be dogged and determined till he gets it."

GRAY WAS IN HIS STUDY, reviewing all the documents from the solicitor, related to his thieving estate manager. The door opened, and he bellowed. "Damn and blast, Devers, I told you no interruptions!"

"Then, it is a very good thing I am not Devers and am not required to listen to you."

Gray tensed at his sister's voice. "I thought you were still cavorting about the continent with your new husband."

Helena smiled. "We've cavorted enough for the time being. I wished to return to Larkland and see about setting that rambling house of his to rights. Speaking of setting things to rights, I've had no less than three people call on me this morning to tell me about your scandalous behavior. Did you really show up here, at our departed granny's home, and install your mistress in this house, right under the noses of everyone? You know that cannot possibly go well."

"I have my reasons," he said. "And, married or not, I do not intend to discuss my mistress, or any other such relationship, with my sister."

She ignored his warning tone and moved closer, settling herself on the corner of his desk. "Edmund, you may be able to fool the rest of the world with your gruff manner, but you and I both know it hides a very tender heart. I would not see some adventuress lead you astray."

A bark of laughter escaped him. "I'd remind you, Helena, that you were running around engaging in all manner of illicit activities with the man who is now your husband prior to taking your vows. Does that make you an adventuress?"

"Of course it doesn't! I love Dudley. I always have," she protested.

"And I love Sabine as she loves me. There are simply complications at the moment that require her to reside under my roof."

"She's not with child?"

For a split second, he wished that she were. It would be a way to tie her to him forever, but even as he thought it, he dismissed it. It would be wrong to limit her choices that way, when they'd been limited so much by others already. "No. But she does face a possible threat, and I have made it my duty to protect her. To that end, I do not wish you to return here until the matter is resolved. I won't have you making a target of yourself."

Helena frowned. "What sort of danger? I do not like this, Edmund. I would not see you hurt for the world."

He settled back in his chair. "You would like her, you know. You already do."

"Who is she, then? No one will say her name. They just say what you have done."

"Madame Sabine de Roussard," he stated, and watched his sister blink in surprise.

"My dressmaker from London?"

"Yes," he answered.

"But she's incredibly successful, Edmund. She does not need you to keep her up. Why would such a woman consent to be any man's mistress?"

His sister's obvious confusion, not to mention her assertion that financial incentives were the only inducement he could provide, were insulting. "I've told you, Helena, the arrangement between us is not what you would think, and it isn't about finances. How low I have sunk that my own sister thinks I cannot draw a woman's eye without flashing a coin at her first!"

"Oh, Edmund, I don't mean it that way, and you know it! But it's a rare thing for a woman in her position, who makes dresses for the creme de la creme of society, to closet herself in the house of her protector, much less to leave behind everything she has worked so hard for, and rusticate in a place like Boston Spa! It will ruin her business, you know. These women who patronize her shop now will not again if they learn of this. They will see this as her attempt to climb the social ladder, and they will not have it."

"Then, damn them all," he said. "If I have my way, I will make her my wife before all is said and done. Scandal be damned, Helena. So, you'd best make your peace with that."

"You really do love her," his sister said in wonderment. "I've never seen you like this."

"I do love her, and I wouldn't wish this torment on my worst enemy."

Helena laughed at that. "It is awful, isn't it? To love someone, to know that they love you, and then to wonder if ever they will be yours. I shall only wish you well, brother. And whether she is to be my sister or not, I will still expect her to make my gowns. She's an artist, you know?"

"I do know," he said.

"What would you have me say to these gossips who seek me out?"

"Nothing," he replied. "It's none of their business."

"Then, I shall go forth in ignorance," Helena offered.

Gray watched her leave and leaned back in his chair. It hadn't taken long at all for news to make the rounds. Bellowing, he shouted, "Devers!"

Moments later, the butler appeared. His face was ashen, and he looked to be on the verge of apoplexy. "Devers, my sister and her husband reside no less than five miles from town. And, yet, already this morning, my sister has been informed by no less than three people that Madame de Roussard is my guest. How do you explain that?"

"I cannot explain it, my lord."

"The only people who knew of her arrival here are the very people who work here, Devers. At what point do the servants in this house have time to gossip about whom I invite to reside under this roof?"

"I could not say, my lord," the butler replied.

"Find out. I want to know who is carrying tales about this household to those who are not part of it."

"Yes, my lord. And, when this loose-tongued person is located, what shall I do with them?"

His first instinct was to see them sacked. But a moment's hesitation brought forth an idea of how their wagging tongues might prove useful. "Bring them to me. I need to know to whom they have spoken. There is a possibility that their gossiping nature may be used to my advantage."

Chapter Thirteen

The delicate tinkling of the bell that hung above the door to the shop heralded the arrival of a customer. Bridget looked up from her work and immediately frowned. They had gentlemen enter the shop from time to time, normally to settle a bill or occasionally to ask for assistance in ensuring that their wives and their mistresses should not cross paths during shopping excursions or fittings.

"May I help you, sir?"

The man offered her a smile, but it was a grotesque expression really. It had nothing to do with the wicked scar at his temple. Rather, it was supremely unnatural. Such a friendly expression had no home on a face like his, not with the coldness that seemed to emanate from him.

"I need to speak with your employer," he said.

"This is my dress shop, sir," Merrilee spoke up

from somewhere behind Bridget. "What is it that we can do for you?"

His expression shifted, becoming almost predatory. "You? You are Madame de Roussard? I think not."

"I have been working here for years, sir. I can assure you that she is Madame de Roussard," Bridget insisted. "Further, I can also state, quite emphatically, that I have never seen you in this shop, and I know that Madame would not entertain a person such as yourself socially."

He started toward her, fists clenched. "A person such as myself? What would a guttersnipe such as you know of quality?"

Bridget removed the pistol that was stored beneath the counter. She'd never before questioned why her employer kept one there, but now she was beginning to see. Raising the weapon high, with the full depth of the shop's counter still between them, she leveled it directly at him. "Not another step, sir. You will vacate these premises, at once."

"She's gone, isn't she? She flew the coop and left you here. Good luck getting a shilling out of the bitch now!" he spat.

But he turned and headed for the door. Bridget rushed forward and locked it after him. Customers or no, she wouldn't risk that man coming in again.

"What on earth possessed you to say you were Madame de Roussard?" she asked Merrilee.

The other girl gestured toward the door. "I saw him. The day that she hired me. He was following her. I was hoping that if I told him I was her, he'd say something to give it away. Who do you think he is?"

Bridget recalled the few times that she'd helped her employer to change gowns or to fit a garment for herself. She'd seen the scars. Not all of them, to be sure, but enough of them to know that the woman had suffered greatly. "Her past come to call. We need to send word to the Earl of Winburn. If she has fled, I hope it's with him."

"Right," Merrilee agreed. "There's a boy works next door. Does deliveries for the apothecary. We can send him. And when you and I leave this shop, we go together. No one travels alone."

Bridgett nodded in agreement, a lead weight of fear settling heavily in her gut. She prayed that the madame was safe. She was much more than just her employer. They were friends, as much as Madame de Roussard was friends with anyone. Guarded from their very first meeting, it was now easy for Bridget to understand why.

⬓

OUTSIDE THE DRESS SHOP, Lawrence fumed. He should have known something was afoot when she hadn't left her house just after sunup to head to her little shop. But he'd get to the bottom of it. He would find where the bitch had run off to. He would not lose track of her again, not when he was so close to freeing himself from the misery of her forever.

Keeping his temper in check while planning to make the strumpets who worked for her pay for their insolence, he could think of only one person who would answer his questions. Hailing a hack, he headed for the home of his wife's lover, the Earl of Winburn.

It was a short journey. When the hack stopped, he tossed a coin to the driver and climbed out. Climbing the steps, he banged the knocker against the door more forcefully than was necessary. Based on the disapproving expression on the pinch-faced butler, it had not gone unnoticed.

"May I help you, sir?"

"I need to see the Earl of Winburn."

"His lordship is not at home." The butler's reply was laced with derision.

He wasn't ignorant of the ways of society. Not at home could mean just that. It could also mean not at home to the likes of him. But if they were both gone, it was a good bet they were gone together. There was only one way to find out. "I was supposed to meet with him before he left for Yorkshire."

"You missed him by a day, sir. Good day to you," the butler said and closed the door.

It had been a guess. Would she return home? Would she try to ruin him? He didn't know. But he'd stop her no matter the cost. But he needed direction. Heading down the street, he turned into the mews and made his way toward the stables. When he saw one of the lads that he recognized as working for Winburn, he called the boy over.

"Boy, what's the name of property that his lordship holds in Yorkshire? I wanted to discuss purchasing the estate from him but hate to sound ill informed."

"Not a name, sir. No estate, either. Just a villa in town at Boston Spa," the lad answered. "You must be thinking of Larkland, which belongs to his brother-in-law."

"That's right. Quite right," Lawrence tossed the lad a coin. "My thanks, young man."

Now he knew where to find the bitch. He'd be on the next mail coach back to Yorkshire.

Chapter Fourteen

It wasn't even noon, and Sabine was half out of her mind with boredom. She'd had a light breakfast in her room after her bath. Following that, she'd obtained embroidery supplies from one of the servants and tried to occupy her hands in the hope that they would in turn occupy her mind. It had failed miserably. To that end, she sought out Gray. He was in his study, furiously working on something.

"What are you doing, and can I possibly offer my assistance with it?"

He looked up. "I didn't realize it was you. I thought it was one of the servants slipping in."

Because she'd learned how to be as unobtrusive as any good servant was while building her business. "Well, I am certainly at your service if you will give me some way to fill my hours. I am not used to being idle, Gray. I require some task, or I will go mad."

His lips quirked. "I see you've given up any pretense of being French."

"My mother was," she admitted. "Though I was so young when she passed that I can hardly remember her at all."

"What other interesting facts about you do I not know?"

She cocked her head to one side as she stepped deeper into the room and trailed her hands along the spines of the books lining the shelves. "I can play the pianoforte and the harp. I am a terrible watercolorist. I do not speak French, but I did manage to learn Latin in secret. My older brother taught me. He'd come home from his tutoring with the rector and then go over all that he'd learned with me that day. We both thought it grossly unfair that he should have to go to school when he did not wish to, while I should be denied going when it was all I wanted."

He smiled at that, clearly amused at the picture she painted. "I see you have always possessed a willful and independent streak."

She truly hadt, though her marriage to Lawrence had certainly quashed it for a while. He'd made her doubt herself, made her questioning and fearful and a shadow of who she once had been. Somehow, in the new identity she'd crafted for herself, she'd rediscovered all the pieces of herself that he'd tried to eradicate with his bullying and abuse. And Gray, for better or worse, was part of that. She'd found her independence and her self-worth on her own, but she'd found her joy with him.

Even as a girl, she hadn't been happy. She simply hadn't been given reasons to be unhappy at that time. The absence of pain was not true happiness. But the man before her, who could love her so gently and so fiercely, who would fight to protect her even from herself, that man had shown her what it meant to truly enjoy living. With him she had learned to savor moments, to let anticipation sweep her into a frenzy. It wasn't simply that their physical relationship was beyond compare. It was in a kiss, an innocent touch, a long and sometimes sly glance. They were connected to one another elementally, as if every part of them had been somehow altered to fit perfectly together. But those were things she could not afford to think of at that moment. Letting her heart hold sway would only see them both hurt.

"What may I do to help you today?"

He sighed. "Can I surmise from the success of your business that you have a decent head for figures?"

"I'm actually very competent," she replied.

He pushed a stack of ledgers toward her. "Then, by all means, balance the account books for this household before I go mad. My sister, when she was residing here, was too busy chasing after the man who would become her husband to pay them any sort of necessary attention."

Taking the books over to a table before the window, she sat down and began working through the first one, column by column. Three columns in, she stopped and asked, "How long has it been since you or your sister resided in this house?"

"Helena technically resided her until three months past, though she was spending most of her time at Larkland, her new husband's estate."

"Then, your servants eat well. *Very* well. As well as Prinny himself, I would daresay," she noted. "They spend an inordinate amount of money at the local butcher shop."

He dropped his own quill, and an expression of extreme annoyance crossed his face. "I'm certain they do. The local butcher hosts bareknuckle fights in the gated yard behind his shop and acts as a bookmaker for those wishing to bet on said fights."

It was Sabine's turn to drop the quill she'd been working with. It clattered to the top of the table from fingers gone numb with nerves. "That's where the fights are held? How near are we to it?"

"It is but two streets over. Nothing in Boston Spa is very far apart. Are you well?"

"I grew up in Doncaster, but Lawrence was from Harrogate. That's where his mills are. He would often come to Boston Spa to bet on those sorts of fights. He'd burned too many bridges in Harrogate, you see. No one there would accept his markers."

GRAY HAD the startling realization that he'd just brought her from the frying pan directly into the fire. But it could be to their benefit. "Then, he will have enemies here. There is no better place for us to be."

"How could it possibly help us? He has the local constabulary and others in power entirely under his thumb!"

"I am not without influence here, Sabine. And if we are to find evidence of his misdeeds, then we must look in the very place where those misdeeds would have occurred."

With another heavy sigh, she rose from the table where the account books were being sorted. "I know that he owed a great deal of money to a gentleman by the name of Mayville."

Gray's eyes widened and a grin spread over his lips. "Not Lord Mayville?"

"He never said. Why? Do you know him?"

"I should say that I do. He's uncle to my sister's husband and a long-standing friend of our family. At one time, I do believe that he had it mind to marry Helena himself, if she would have had him."

"Is it really possible that I ran all the way to London only to put myself squarely within his reach by entangling myself with a man indirectly connected to him?" She demanded incredulously.

Gray nodded slightly. "So it would seem. Do you

know what this smacks of, Sabine? It is fate. It can be nothing but fate. Had you ever doubted we were destined for one another, this should disabuse you of that notion."

She walked toward him, settled her bottom on the edge of his desk, and clasped her hands in front of her. She looked down at them for the longest moment. "I concede that it seems as if it could be nothing else. So, what do we do now?"

"We are going to pay a visit to Mayville. And he should be able to point us in the direction of others who will offer up what we need."

"And if he's not committed or we cannot prove a hanging offense? What then?"

He would kill him. She would be free of Lawrence Russell if it was the last thing he did, by any means necessary. "Let us cross that bridge when we come to it."

Chapter Fifteen

Gray sent a note round to Lord Mayville that afternoon. A footman had been dispatched in return, with
an invitation for the pair of them to dine with him
that evening. And, so, they'd taken the carriage late in
the afternoon, traveling the few miles between his villa
in town and Lord Mayville's estate, Rosedale Manor.
As they arrived, Gray noted that the house was
unchanged from his last visit. Mayville had often
expressed his contempt for his ancestral home and
that he intended to let it fall to ruin until it crumbled
to dust. He appeared to be sticking to his word on the
matter.

A butler answered the door and ushered them into
a drawing room. Gray spared a glance toward Sabine.
She appeared utterly terrified, as if she wished to look
under and rebind every stick of furniture for fear that

Russell was lying in wait for her. Gray placed his hand over hers where it rested on his arm.

"It's fine. Mayville is a friend," he offered quietly.

"Friends are a luxury I have not permitted myself," she replied.

He didn't reply. Mayville entered at that moment. On the surface, the man appeared a dissolute rake. But Gray knew the truth of it. Despite his statement that he might have married Helena, Mayville had been nursing a broken heart for more than a decade. The woman he loved had chosen another and set him on a path of ruin.

"It's good to see you," Gray said, the moment his friend entered.

"And you," Mayville said. "But this is hardly an impromptu visit, is it? And you, madame, are very familiar to me."

"We've never met," Sabine answered.

Mayville's lips quirked upward. "No, indeed. We have not. But I have seen your face, nonetheless. Your allegedly bereaved husband had put posters all over Yorkshire with your face on them. Abducted by brigands, were you, Mrs. Russell?"

Gray felt Sabine stiffen beside him. Interceding, he cautioned his friend, "Mayville, do not. The man is a brute, as I'm certain you can well imagine if you are as acquainted with him as I have been led to believe."

Mayville offered a laconic shrug and then stepped deeper into the room. "Sherry?"

"Brandy, if you have it," Sabine stated, her voice never quavering.

Mayville chuckled. "I like you. A woman who flees brutality and shirks convention. What is it that you need of me?"

"Information," Gray said. "What sort of misdeeds has Russell been involved with that would see the man swinging by a noose?"

Mayville walked over to them, two glasses of brandy in hand. "He's done everything, Gray. Rape, murder, theft, embezzlement… But this is not a man who will ever be made to hang. Not in Yorkshire. He operates textile mills that employ half the populations of several towns and villages. They will shelter and protect him regardless of how little he deserves it."

"I told you." Sabine's admonition was offered softly. "He has the power here because others are dependent upon him. The longer we are here, the more we are at risk."

"I wouldn't say that," Mayville said. "Not everyone is dependent upon him. I hold a not-insignificant number of his markers. I can have him thrown into debtor's prison. A man of his age and health would likely die in such a place."

"It would buy us time. It would also allow you to assume ownership of the mills," Gray stated. "Would you dirty your hands with trade?"

Mayville laughed. "I'll dirty my hands with anything that will see the ancestors rolling in their graves, you know that! Let us enjoy our dinner, and I will plot and plan his demise for you. And we shall drink a not-insignificant amount of wine, and you all shall stay the night. My servants have been hired precisely because they do not possess prudish natures."

Gray did not agree or disagree. He would leave that to Sabine to decide later. Following Mayville into the dining room, he shook his head at the man's opulence. The table was laden for a feast, while the frescoes on the ceiling crumbled and silk peeled from the wall.

"I see you are true to your word. You mean to let it crumble around you until naught is left," Gray observed.

"I do. This place is naught but a monument to misery. The sooner it collapses, the better." There was a long-standing animosity between Mayville and his disapproving relatives. The house was a bone of contention between them all.

"Tell me, Mrs. Russell, is your husband here in Yorkshire, or did he track you to London and find you in the arms of my friend?" Mayville asked, gesturing with a flourish to the footmen that they should begin serving.

"I suppose I would have to say it's the latter, but I beg of you, do not call me that. For the last several years I have lived happily under the name Sabine de

Roussard. It feels much more natural to me than Mrs. Russell ever did."

"Sabine," he said, rolling the name on his tongue rather like he was tasting the wine. "It suits you. And, as I have no manners, wretched breeding, and am forever told that I am incorrigible, I shall simply call you that. You may call Mayville if you choose, or you may call me Sinclair. That is my given name. Few enough are granted permission, but you, my dear, are deserving."

"Because I flouted convention and left my abusive husband?" She asked.

"No. Because you've captured the heart of one of my oldest friends…and because you nearly killed your abusive husband before you took off. It was you, I presume. That tail of a burglar coming in through the window was always a bit difficult to take."

Gray watched Sabine closely, wondering how she would react to Mayville's flirtation and to his somewhat exaggerated persona. The man was not so dissolute as he presented himself to be. Gray knew for a fact that his honor was unimpeachable. But Sabine simply offered a cool smile and kept her secrets. It was her standard response to everything.

Mayville shrugged and grinned, turning his attention to Gray in that moment. "As I see it, we have two options: I can call in his markers and see him tossed into a debtor's prison…or, Gray, I can sign those markers over to you and you can make a trade. The markers would be returned in exchange for his agreement to an annulment. Presuming, of course, that you can sway the House of Lords to your cause."

"I can. It will be time consuming. And one must also consider whether the man would honor any agreement that was made," Gray mused. "My understanding of his character lends me to believe he would agree and immediately renege."

"That is not an unfounded opinion," Mayville agreed. "Let me think on it. I may yet have more to offer in this situation. In the meantime, let us eat, drink, and be merry. We can discuss what a grand chase your sister is leading my nephew on. But for the grace of God, there go I!"

***

WINE FLOWED FREELY THROUGH DINNER. So freely that, by the time the meal was at an end, Sabine knew they must accept Mayville's hospitality. She did hope, however, that the bedchambers were in better repair than the public areas of the house. No one presumed to put them in separate rooms. She and Gray were shown to a single chamber to share.

Looking around, Sabine was relieved to see the bedchambers were in better condition than the rest of the house. The paint and wallpaper were peeling and the curtains faded, but everything appeared quite sound.

"It's almost as if we are married," he said, as they entered.

She smirked. "I should think that, if married women enter Lord Mayville's abode, they do so without their husbands."

Gray chuckled softly. "I would not disagree with your assessment. But I like being here with you. Free from judgement, free from gossip. No one here cares about your past."

"I thought he was dead, you now," she admitted. "I really believed that I had killed him. I never intended to be an adulteress. But I never intended to be a murderess, either. My life has taken so many unexpected turns. And as horrible as some of them have been, I can't regret a thing, because it's brought me here to you."

Gray stepped closer to her, folding her into his arms. "I feel the same."

"Ask me," Sabine blurted out.

"Ask you what?"

"The question you wished to ask me. The question which had you walking around with a ridiculously large sapphire ring in your pocket. Ask me."

He blinked in surprise. "I didn't think that was a question you wanted to answer."

She hadn't either. But in that moment of brilliant clarity, something had shifted for her. In all her denials of why it could never work, of why she would never allow him to damage himself by tying himself to her, she'd never considered how much damage she might do by severing those bonds. Because in all of it, she hadn't allowed herself to believe that he could possibly love her as much as she loved him. It was a disservice to them both. "I may never be free to carry through on it. I realize that. And I need you to understand that, as well. But I want to give you the answer from my heart…the one that I hope and pray we can fulfill together."

He didn't ask any further questions. He closed the distance between them and dropped to one knee. One hand slipped into the inside pocket of his coat, and he produced a small leather box.

"You kept it with you?" she asked in wonderment.

"I wanted to be prepared," he replied. Flipping open the tiny latch, the lid lifted back to reveal a large sapphire. He'd described it as the size of a robin's egg, and he had not been wrong. The center stone was flanked by diamonds and pearls, while the heavy gold band that held the king's ransom in stones was ornately carved and incredibly beautiful.

"Sabine de Roussard…Sally Russell…by any name you care to call yourself, will you be my wife?" he asked.

"Why?"

"Because in all my life, I've never loved a woman the way that I love you. You are my once in a lifetime," he admitted with complete vulnerability.

"I love you, Gray. I love you more than I can

possibly say, and I want nothing more than to be your wife. God willing, we will find a way to make it happen," she stated.

"I'm not content to sit back and wait for the Almighty," Gray said, slipping the ring on her finger before getting to his feet. "I mean to end this, Sabine, one way or another. You will be free of him no matter what."

Her heart stuttered in her chest. "You scare me when you say those things. He's a dangerous man, Gray. He's dangerous, and he has no honor. You cannot challenge him to a duel to make this go away. Promise me you will not!"

"I don't intend to. I intend to see him hang for his crimes," Gray replied emphatically. "Trust me, Sabine. Trust me to keep you safe."

"If anyone can, it would be you," she admitted.

Chapter Sixteen

Gray kissed her. It wasn't simply hunger. It was desperation and fear. Despite his assurances, he understood what they were up against, and it terrified him. There was no mistaking that she felt the same. She clung to him with the same kind of need, to hold on, to feel secure in that moment.

As always, the need became overwhelming. It superseded everything else—even fear. As the heat built between them, rising to a fever pitch, all the worries and fears simply fell away. As long as he could hold her, all was right in the world for that moment.

Lifting her into his arms, he bore her back to the bed. Clothes fell away. Teeth and tongues clashed as questing hands explored. It was explosive. Incendiary. It was furious and hungry. It left them breathless and weak in the aftermath, clinging to one another like warriors locked in battle.

But even when the pleasure had receded, he didn't let go of her. He held her closely, protectively.

"I"m not going anywhere. I won't leave you," she said.

"Good. I don't intend to let you," he said.

She snuggled against him, pressing her cheek to his chest. "I do love you. I never knew pleasure like this was possible. I had never experience anything with a man but pain and humiliation, until you. You've given me the world, Gray, whatever else happens."

Gray stroked her back and shoulders, feeling the ridges of scars there. He continued to do so even as she drifted off to sleep. When he knew that she was well and truly settled for the night, he retrieved his breeches and shirt and went in search of Mayville. His friend knew things he had not said. It had been a subtle thing, the look Mayville had cast him as they'd parted ways after dinner.

Downstairs, he heard the clattering of billiard balls. Making his way to the billiard room, he found Mayville inside. There was a bottle of brandy and glasses on the table by the door, so he helped himself to it.

"I'm going to kill him," Mayville said.

"You can't do that."

"On the contrary, I can. He cheated at cards."

"You can afford the loss," Gray said. It struck him then, the irony of trying to save Russell's life. But it was Mayville's soul he was more concerned about it.

"It wasn't me he cheated against. It was Lottie's younger brother. He ruined the boy, took his entire inheritance. And then he took his own life," Mayville explained.

"You don't owe her anything," Gray said. "She left you for another."

"I cannot help but believe there are extenuating circumstances," Mayville insisted. "And I swore an oath to love her for all of our lives."

"But not in church. She walked away from you before that could happen."

Mayville's lips quirked in a wry smile. "So she did. But my oath was not contingent upon hers. Tell me, Gray, if your Sabine left you, would the love simply stop because she'd married another? Her being married to another didn't stop it from developing, after all."

"That wasn't a marriage, it was a prison sentence," he protested. "But, no, I would not stop loving her. Not for any reason."

"Then, there you have it. What a pair of hopeless romantics we are!"

"Not hopeless. Unfairly optimistic, perhaps."

Mayville lifted his glass. "To optimism, then."

Gray raised his in return. "Does she know?"

"Does she know what?"

"That you pine for her," Gray stated.

Mayville shrugged. "I like to think we are both pining separately for one another. That damnable optimism again."

⬛

LAWRENCE RUSSELL OBTAINED a room at the Farrer's Hotel. The young man who showed him to his room was only about fifteen. The boy would be glad enough for a coin to spill all that he knew. So, Lawrence began peppering him with questions.

"Have you heard that the Earl of Winburn is in town?"

The boy looked back at him and nodded. "Aye, I've heard that, sir."

"And that he brought his doxy with him," Lawrence tested.

"I don't talk about my betters, sir. I've been taught not to gossip. My sweet mother would never permit such talk in her house," the boy insisted.

"It isn't gossip to tell the truth, boy. The earl is here, and he has a woman with him. If you confirm that for me, or even deny it truthfully, I'll give you a guinea."

The boy sighed heavily. "I heard the kitchen girls say that he come up from London with a woman. I don't know nothing else about it."

Lawrence, as promised, handed him the coin. "That's all I require. These kitchen girls, did they see them together, perhaps?"

"I don't know, sir."

"Find out and there's another guinea for you. Better yet, bring one of those girls to speak with me so I may ask her myself. And then I'll give you both a guinea."

The lad gripped the coin tightly in his fist, seemed to weigh the money against his conscience. After a moment, he gave a curt nod and walked away, leaving Lawrence alone before the door to his hotel room.

Stepping into the chamber, he didn't have anything to do but take a seat near the window and wait. He had no bags to unpack or see to. It was simply a matter of waiting for information.

Moments later, the same young lad knocked on his door. He had a young girl with him, near his own age. She had mousy hair tucked into a cap and a dirty apron on over an equally dowdy dress.

"You are one of the kitchen girls who spoke of the earl and his light skirt?"

The serving girl blushed. "I don't wish to speak ill of no one."

Reaching into the pocket of his coat, Lawrence removed the small miniature that had been painted of Sally during their marriage. He waved in front of the girl's face "Is this the woman who is with him?"

The girl took the miniature. "Could be, sir. It were dark when they arrived by coach. But it do look like her."

"And where did they go? Where is the earl's villa here in town?"

"It's two streets over, near the church," the girl answered.

Producing the guineas as promised, he delivered one to each of them. "That is all I require from you now. You may go."

———

OUTSIDE THE DOOR, the boy looked at the kitchen girl. "I don't like him, Bennie. He's got cold eyes."

"We could warn his lordship that the man's asking questions. My cousin works in the kitchens there. What's his name?"

"Family name is Russell," the boy said. "I heard him say it when he checked in."

"We could warn them, Davie. His lordship, I mean. My cousin works in the kitchens there. And I know her face. That woman in the painting…she's been missing for a long time. Saw posters all over town before, asking for information 'bout her and offering a reward."

"Don't pay no mind to those things, myself. Can't read 'em no way."

"I don't feel right about him. Not at all," she said.

"Talk to your cousin. I'll cover for you."

Bennie nodded and then slipped down the stairs. It would not take her long to get there and speak to Cora.

Chapter Seventeen

They were in the breakfast room, another ramshackle and dilapidated chamber at Lord Mayville's estate. But, as she'd come to expect, the food was excellent, and the servants were discreet and respectful. There was a story there—something in the way he reviled his family estate yet refused to leave it—that intrigued her.

"A missive arrived for you this morning, Gray," Mayville said, entering the room. He looked a bit worse for wear, his pallor indicating a night of excess.

"The only people who know we are here are my servants," Gray said.

And they would only interrupt their visit with Lord Mayville for something important. Something that would likely, she thought, be considered a threat. That could mean that Lawrence had found them.

"He's here, isn't he?" Sabine asked.

Gray said nothing at first, simply opened the missive and scanned the contents. Then he looked up. "So it would seem. He's at the Farrar's Hotel. I had not expected that he would arrive so quickly."

"He was watching us in London. He would have noticed when I failed to turn up at my shop," Sabine observed. "And even the most loyal servants can inadvertently reveal information, especially if they feel it is an insignificant piece of information."

"That is all very true," Mayville concurred. "I would advise that, at this point, the safest course of action would be to send you, Madame Sabine de Roussard, to Larkland. As horrible as it will be for you to be parted from your love for a time, it is necessary for the next step to take place."

"I think that is an excellent notion. I can't do what is necessary to see you safe, Sabine, if I am worried about you all the time. I can trust you will be safe at Larkland. I can have your things sent over, or I'm certain Helena would be happy to provide what you might require from her own not-insignificant wardrobe," Gray stated.

Sabine eyed the two men in the room. There was something there, an undercurrent passing between them. They both knew something they were not telling her. Did she want to know? That was the ultimate question. She trusted Gray, and because she trusted him, she felt compelled to extend that trust to Lord Mayville.

"You're planning something, and you are intentionally keeping it from me," she guessed.

"Yes," Mayville replied. "And I do not intend to alter that situation. I have my own issues to settle with Lawrence Russell. The outcome will be to your benefit, I assure you. And your betrothed will be safe the entire time, I promise you that. You need do nothing but stay out of my way."

"And you, Lord Mayville? Will you be in danger?" Sabine asked. It was a short acquaintance, but Lord Mayville had quickly become one of the few people in the world she permitted herself to care for. She felt, to the depth of her soul, that he was also not a man very many people had cared for in his life, though he had certainly deserved better.

"A modicum of danger, perhaps. But I assure you, when all is said and done, you will be a widow in truth rather than fiction," he vowed.

"But I don't want you to put yourself in danger," she insisted. "I think you do so because you imagine that no one would mourn at the loss of you. And you could not be more wrong."

Lord Mayville stared at her for the longest moment, his expression inscrutable. When at last he spoke, his tone was soft, "My dearest, Sabine, were Winburn not my only friend, I would steal you from him at this very moment. As it is, I will wish you both the most happiness together that two people may ever know. And I promise that I shall toast you at your wedding breakfast."

Gray took her hand, his thumb sweeping over the weight of the ring he'd placed on her finger the night before. "I've asked you to trust me, Sabine. Now I need you to show me that you do. Go to Larkland. Stay under guard with Helena until I return there for you."

"I don't like this."

"You don't have to like it," Gray said. "I simply need you to agree. Please."

What could she do? In essence, it was time to prove that she believed in him, rather than simply stating that she did. After years of being on her own, of constantly looking over her shoulder, this man she had come to love so dearly was asking her to prove her faith in him and let her end the fear that had been her constant companion. "I will, if you promise not to make me regret it. I can live without many things in my life, Gray. But you are not one of them."

"After this short-but-necessary absence, we will never be apart again," he vowed.

"Then, summon your carriage and send me to Larkland, before I change my mind," she said.

"I took the liberty," Mayville said. "It's waiting for you when you are ready. I'll leave you a moment to say your goodbyes."

When Mayville had exited the room, Sabine didn't wait for Gray to speak. Instead, she simply stepped closer to him, wrapped her arms about him, and held on. "Do not say goodbye to me. I cannot bear it."

"Then, I will not," he agreed, his hand stroking her back as he held her for the moment. "I promise you all will be well, and this will be at an end. You will be free of him, and we will be free to start our life together."

"I should go. The longer I stay with you, the harder it is to walk away. You've informed your sister I am to stay with her?"

"I did. I sent a note round to her this morning that I would be sending you to her when things came to a head. I did not realize that would be today, however."

"Fine. When will I see you again?"

"I think tomorrow," he said. "This will resolve quickly."

Sabine looked at him once more and then did the hardest thing she ever had: She turned and walked away.

GRAY WATCHED HER WALK OUT, feeling his heart sinking as she did so. He wasn't challenging Russell himself, as he had promised her he would not. But there would be a duel, and he would be part of it.

Mayville entered as soon as Sabine exited. He wore no cravat nor waistcoat but had donned his coat over his shirt, which hung open at the neck. "I've had two mounts saddled. I assume you would like to meet the social standard and change out of your rumpled evening clothes?"

"It would be nice to do so, yes," Gray agreed. "We need to wait for Dudley, as well. I sent a note round to him this morning that I needed to speak with him. Will he serve as second to Russell?"

Mayville shrugged. "Perhaps. I doubt that Russell will permit it. He will likely summon one of the gentlemen who frequent the fights the butcher hosts. There are several who live close by. But having Dudley there when the challenge is issued will be to our benefit."

"He'll cry foul regardless," Gray pointed out. "Based on what I know of him, he appears to be very gifted at finding others to blame for his misfortune."

"It's a talent he has cultivated over many years. What happened when she left? I do not believe the story he bandied about that they interrupted a house-breaker, who then attacked him and abducted her. Clearly, she left of her own accord."

Gray shrugged. "That is not my story to tell. Suffice to say if you shoot him, it will be no less than he deserves. The man is the worst sort of brute and bully. He deserves whatever fate hands to him."

"Fate will hand him a pistol ball. A fatal one," Mayville said. "Let's head to town before it gets any later. I'd like to get this done and all the arrangements in place so that there's no chance of him absconding beforehand."

"You think he'd be cowardly enough to run?"

Mayville nodded. "I've little doubt of it. And I've made a promise to your fair Sabine. It only punctuates the other vows I have made. I cannot allow him to slip through my hands."

Gray clenched his fists at his side. "I wish I could be the one to end his miserable life."

Mayville turned for the door. "I'm rather shocked you didn't protest more. Why is that? It isn't cowardice, I'm certain. But I've little doubt you've a well thought out reason."

"If I kill him, people will never let it go. It will always seem as if she was just a cheating wife and I the dupe she seduced into ending her miserable marriage. The gossips will never leave her alone," Gray mused. "I do not want her to ever have reason to regret being my wife."

"And you think a bit of gossip might? You clearly do not know the lady's heart," Mayville noted.

Gray shrugged. "It isn't worth the risk, not when there is another way and you are so determined."

"There's more."

A heavy sigh escaped him. "I do not want Sabine to connect us in her mind. I do not want her to ever look at me and think of him, and if I am the one to end his life, it links us forever."

"Then let us see this done—for the good of us both."

Chapter Eighteen

Lawrence had slept later than intended, likely helped along by the large amount of brandy he'd consumed. It hadn't been good brandy, but it was the best he could come by. He'd dressed quickly in his rumpled clothes, meaning to make his way to the villa that the Earl of Winburn called home in the sleepy village of Boston Spa. He'd no sooner tied his cravat than a knock sounded on his door.

Assuming it was the lad from the previous night there to sell a bit more info for another coin, he quickly yanked the door open and was greeted with three men whom he hadn't realized were connected. The Earl of Winburn stood there, next to Lord Mayville, to whom he owed a not-insignificant amount of money. And the third gentleman with them, Mr. Dudley Blakemore, had all the evidence any person needed to see him hang.

It was Blakemore who spoke first. "Lawrence Russell, I am here on behalf of Lord Mayville to issue a challenge. Pistols at dawn, in the fallow just below the bridge. As you've no second, should you choose to accept this challenge, I will serve for you."

"And if I choose not to accept?" Lawrence bluffed.

Blakemore smiled. "We both know that isn't an option. You will accept Lord Mayville's challenge, or you will swing."

"Fine. Dawn it is," he snapped. His gaze turned toward Winburn. "She's a faithless bitch. You'll never get a son out of her."

Winburn raised an eyebrow at that. "You've had three wives, Russell, and never gotten a son out of any of them. It's not a stretch to imagine that the women are not the problem."

Lawrence could feel his blood boiling at that. But he was outnumbered and outmatched, a fact that he well knew. If it had been but one of them, he'd have acted very differently, to be sure.

"Gentleman," Dudley Blakemore said, "if you would wait at the end of the corridor, I would have a private word with Mr. Russell."

"I've got nothing to say to you," Lawrence replied.

"Then, it will be a short and very one-sided conversation," Blakemore replied, as the two other men moved to the end of the hall.

"Speak and be done with it, then!"

"I have it, Russell. I have all the proof that is required to see you ruined. Your business was obtained through illegal means. You abducted and married the daughter of your business partner and then murdered him so you could inherit. And, when it was convenient, you rid yourself of her."

"What business is it of yours if I did?"

"Then there is that other matter, about the weapons that were paced between bolts of cloth and shipped off to France during the war. Treason may be profitable, but it carries a steep penalty."

Lawrence felt his gut clench. How did he know? "You can't prove it!"

"But I can. You see, I intercepted one of your shipments while I was working in intelligence in France during the war. Imagine my surprise when I saw a group of Frenchmen unloading a shipment of English cloth. And when I dug through the one of those crates myself, I found musket parts. English musket parts. I saw it with my own eyes. How many Englishmen did you help kill, Russell?"

"So superior those who were born with everything can afford to be!" Lawrence snapped. "If you'd had to fight for everything you have, as I did, you'd be singing a different tune!"

"I might," Blakemore admitted. "But it wouldn't be bloody French. I have proof, Russell, of your treason and more. I make it a point to gather information. I've devoted my life to it. I happened to stumble upon yours in the pursuit of something else. But I kept it because it could prove valuable. And I say that now because there is a way out, Russell, that doesn't involve a duel or a noose. You'll be humiliated, your memory scorned, and the world will know you for the wretch that you are. Unless you were to suffer some unfortunate accident while cleaning your pistols in advance of some sport shooting with a group of gentlemen. It would be the easiest way, wouldn't it?"

"Easiest for you, not for me," Lawrence snapped.

Blakemore shrugged. "You may survive the duel. But you won't survive the noose. Do you really want that looming over you? Arrests, public humiliation, confiscation of everything you've worked for by the crown—there are worse things than death, Russell. Think on it."

"What is in this for you?"

Blakemore cocked his head to one side. "There are few people in my life whom I care for. My uncle, Lord Mayville, is one of them. And, since I am married to the earl's sister, it behooves me to aid in his happiness that I may protect my own. In short, Russell, I possess the ability to care for others. It is something completely foreign to you, I think."

Lawrence stepped back and slammed the door, shutting out the other man's smug face. It goaded him that the bastard was right. Even if he survived the duel (which was unlikely, given what he knew of

Mayville), the humiliation that would follow would destroy him. When he considered what was to come, having all his worldly possessions confiscated, of being tried in public and all his dirty secrets trotted out for everyone to see—he couldn't do it. There really was only one option, but it required more nerve than he possessed at the moment.

Glancing back at the table, half the bottle of wretched brandy remained from the night before. It should do. For what he needed, it should do.

AT THE END of the corridor, Mayville at his side, Gray watched his brother-in-law walking towards them. There was much more to Dudley Blakemore than the affable and unassuming gentleman of means that he presented. It was something he'd always been aware of: the undercurrent of danger, the way the man seemed to observe everything around him.

"What did you say to him?" Gray demanded.

"I simply pointed out that his past misdeeds could come to light and that, even if he did manage victory on the morrow, it would be short-lived glory for him when the constables come for him. And that if he didn't wish to die in a duel or by the noose, there was another option."

Mayville stiffened beside him. "He'll take the

coward's way out. You've deprived me of the oppor-tunity to avenge a young man whom he exploited!"

"It isn't your place to avenge him," Blakemore pointed out. "You are my uncle, one of the few family members I have left. You are certainly the only one who deigns to acknowledge me, given how lowly my mother married. If you need not jeopardize yourself to achieve the same outcome—ridding the world of a man who adds nothing to it with his presence—then why should you?"

"If he does do this," Gray said, "it will be so much better for everyone. But, for our benefit, we need to be seen leaving this hotel, en masse, before it occurs. To that end, we should leave now."

"Always the voice of reason," Blakemore agreed. "Let us depart quickly."

The three of them made it down the narrow stair-case and into the main area of the hotel. Gray watched as Dudley made it a point to smile and offer polite greetings to others present. It only begged further question as to what exactly his brother-in-law had done during the war. He knew that Dudley was decorated, that he'd received multiple commenda-tions, but the nature of his service had always been mysterious. Gray was beginning to understand why.

"Where to now?"

"Some place with an audience, no doubt," Mayville offered with a very gallic shrug.

"Are you that disappointed at not having been put in a position to kill or be killed?" Gray demanded.

"Maybe I did want to be her hero," Mayville offered with a twisted smirk. "Maybe I begrudge losing an opportunity to make her regret her own choices once more."

Gray thought carefully about how to phrase his suggestion. "Perhaps you would do better to look at finding a new love, rather than striving to maintain connections with one who moved on from you?"

"Old dogs, Winburn, and new tricks."

Having returned from his efforts to make their departure noteworthy, Blakemore suggested a pin in the local tavern. Nodding his agreement, Gray followed his brother-in-law and friend from the hotel. He couldn't quite bring himself to pray that Russell would take Blakemore's guarded suggestion. But it didn't stop that dark hope from springing up inside him. He simply wanted her to be free, not just to marry him, but to live without fear. She deserved that at least, regardless of anything else.

Chapter Nineteen

Arriving at Larkland in Gray's carriage had been quite the experience. While everyone in the house was unfailingly polite, there was clearly some confusion as to what anyone should make of her. A dressmaker treated as an exalted guest, arriving in a carriage that belonged to the Earl of Winburn, and without a single possession to her name. There were certainly better ways to make an entrance, but it was memorable to say the least.

Seated at a small dressing table in her chamber while the newly wedded Lady Helena Blakemore nee Grayson began sorting through the selection of gowns that had been brought in by her maid and laid upon the bed. She held up a bottle-green day dress.

"This should do nicely for today," Lady Helena observed.

It should indeed. She'd made the blasted thing.

But Sabine didn't say that. Instead, she simply smiled and nodded. "Yes, it will be lovely. Thank you."

Lady Helena looked at the dress once more and then a blush crept over her cheeks. "We're in a very strange sort of predicament here, aren't we?"

"It is unusual," Sabine agreed.

"Do you love my brother?"

The question was impertinent, blurted out impulsively, and yet there was no apology. Only concern was etched on Lady Helena's face.

"I do," Sabine answered. "I love him more than anything."

"Enough to let him go?"

Deciding that honesty was the best course, Sabine answered with complete transparency. "If it was best for him, yes. But I do not think it is. I've come to learn something about him: He is very determined. And he sees us having a life together. Even if I could summon the altruism to walk away from him—which is difficult to imagine, since I, too, very much want that life—he wouldn't let me. He'd follow me to the ends of the earth. I don't have it in me to make him live that way… And I find that, after years of misery, I'm unwilling to live that way myself. I deserve to be happy. I deserve to be loved. And I am both when I am with him."

Still clutching the day dress, Lady Helena sank down onto the bench at the foot of the bed. "I have to confess that, in all the times I visited your shop, I never really saw you. I physically saw you, of course…but not as a person. You made beautiful gowns that I wished to wear. The idea that you had any sort of life outside of that setting never dawned on me. It certainly would never have entered my mind to think that you were carrying on an affair with my brother while I was a patron in your shop!"

It would truly scandalize her to know of the many times Gray was in the small apartment above the shop while she had been browsing the wares one floor below. But sharing that would hardly help the situation, so Sabine wisely kept it to herself. "That is the way our society works. In truth, I counted on that. By going into a trade, as it were, I gave myself a kind of invisibility I would never have had otherwise. It is what allowed me to escape him for so long."

"What did he do to you?" Helena asked.

"It would be easier to start with what he did not. He did not allow me to have dignity or security. He did not allow me to live without fear on any given day that I might be beaten or brutalized or punished for some imagined infraction. I had no independence, and I had no safety. I had no happiness and no joy. It was all pain, fear, uncertainty and humiliation. Every day of my life with him."

"And is that why you left? Because he beat you?"

"I left," Sabine replied, "because he determined that I'd outlived my usefulness to him, and he was going to force me to consume a lethal dose of laudanum. I left because, as miserable as my life had been, I still was not ready to see it end."

"So, you embarked on this affair with my brother, still married to this other gentleman, with no notion that you would ever become his countess?"

"I didn't know I was still married. There was a terrible struggle on the night I fled. I thought I had killed him. But I couldn't be sure. And I couldn't ask too many questions without jeopardizing the life I had built for myself. My assumption was that I was either still married or a murderess, and either of those would prohibit any furthering of my relationship with your brother. But he is very persuasive."

Helena sighed. Laying the dress down on the bed, she smoothed the creases she had just put in it. "I don't want you to think that I am only concerned about the scandal. I'm not. I simply want to know that whatever scandal we weather will be worth it. That you truly love him and will make him happy."

"My love is without question. My greatest fear is that he will marry me and then determine it was not worth the cost," Sabine admitted.

Helena smiled. "I do not think you need worry on that score. My brother has a remarkable ability to be the most single-minded man on the face of this earth. He determines what is important to him without regard for what might matter to anyone else. I quote him directly when I say, 'society be damned.'"

It was Sabine's turn to smile. "I've heard him say it as well."

"Then, believe it. Because if he says it doesn't matter, it does not. He will not permit it."

A knock on the door interrupted their conversation. A servant entered, bearing a silver tray with a folded bit of paper on it.

"What is it?" Helena asked nervously.

"It is for Madame de Roussard, from the Earl of Winburn, my lady," the footman replied.

Helena waved him on, and he approached Sabine with the tray. She didn't want to take it. She didn't want to read the letter and find out if something horrible had occurred. With a shaking hand, she accepted the missive and broke the simple wax seal. Scanning the quite predictably brief script, it took her a moment to process what had been relayed.

"What is it?" Helenda demanded. The silence had stretched to a point of discomfort for her.

Sabine looked back at the note and then simply read it aloud. "*R.L. has taken his own life, rather than risk the field of honor or punishment for his crimes. We will return to Larkland by evening.*"

Helena let out a shriek of frustration. "That man! Does he never use words?"

Sabine considered it. He did. He used them all the time. Funny, biting, witty, heartfelt…but not written. Everything he expressed, he did so while looking one directly in the eyes. Forthright and forthcoming, it was simply his way. "It's over. It's really over. I am now what I longed to be from my wedding night forward: a widow."

Helena drew in a breath sharply. "I suppose the question remains whether or not you are willing to be a bride again, doesn't it?"

GRAY SLOWED his mount as he neared the grand front doors to Larkland. He'd sent a message on ahead to apprise Sabine of Russell's fate because he hadn't wanted her to worry. They'd remained close to town for a bit longer to plant the seed that it had been an accident rather than suicide. He didn't know whether she wished to resume her life as Sally Russell or if she'd continue on as Sabine de Roussard. But he wished for her to have both options available.

Dismounting easily, his booted feet crunched on the graveled drive as he crossed the short distance to the wide front steps. The heavy mahogany doors with their Moorish arch opened silently as he neared them. But it wasn't the butler who greeted him. It was his sister.

"Stop right there," she said. "We need a word before you enter this house."

"I mean to marry her, Helena. I couldn't care less for the scandal," he said with exasperation.

"And I want you to marry her, Gray. You love her,

and she loves you, I think more than you realize," Helena said softly. "But you cannot expect her to be widowed in one day and wed the next."

"She had no love for him. He made her life a misery when they were together, and she's lived in fear of him since she fled into the night," he insisted hotly.

"Yes. And, in all that time, all she wanted was her freedom. I'm suggesting, my dearest brother, that unless you give her a moment to take that breath of freedom, you may drive her away. Give her a moment's peace. Give her a chance to fully acclimate to all that has occurred. If you love her, is another month or two really so much to wait?"

"I can't be without her for that long." It was a jagged admission, something broken and desperate that he hated to admit to anyone.

"And you shouldn't be. Be with her. Love her as you always have. But allow things to stand as they are just for a time," Helena urged. "I would not see you hurt for the world. No one knows as well as I do that you do not give your heart lightly. If she has it, she'll have it forever. Just let her breathe. Because if you ask her to run away with you, to elope and marry you tomorrow, she will because hurting you would break her heart. But she could resent you for it later."

There was nothing Helena had said that he had not thought himself. Those doubts had been plaguing him from the moment he rode out of Boston Spa toward

Larkland. Was she ready? Would finally having her freedom from Russell change her mind? Would she still need him? It was an incessant litany of desperation.

"Fine. I'll speak to her about taking our time and…adjusting to her new status."

"You won't regret it. I promise you," Helena said. She then rose on her toes and kissed his cheek. "Now, go get yourself cleaned up. I could not place you in adjoining chambers. The servants would be scandalized. But you are conveniently just across the hall from her."

When Helena had retreated inside, he stood there for a moment and considered everything. He could wait. Not indefinitely, but for her, he could wait a bit longer.

Entering the house, he climbed the stairs to his room and, per his sister's direction, cleaned himself up. When he didn't look like he'd just climbed off the back of a horse, he stepped out into the corridor. Seeing no one about, he strode to Sabine's door and knocked softly. She called out, bidding him to enter, and he did so.

She was at her dressing table, pinning her hair up in some elaborate style for dinner. But the moment she saw him, it was forgotten. She let the strands she'd been working with fall from her fingers, and she rushed toward him, all but hurtling herself into his waiting arms.

"You didn't challenge him," she guessed. "But Lord Mayville did."

"Mayville had his own bone to pick with Lawrence Russell. So did Blakemore, it seems. If I'd been aware of who he was and the threat he posed months ago, we could have avoided so much worry and unnecessary suffering. Please, Sabine, do not keep secrets from me again. My poor heart cannot withstand it."

She gave a watery chuckle. "Nor mine. And, while your sister has been inordinately kind, the sooner we can make for London and our life there, the happier I will be. I'm not a fan of Yorkshire anymore."

"Do you wish to see your family while we are here?" He asked.

"No. I wrote my father once. I risked everything and reached out to him. He sent the letter back to me through the agent I had hired and encouraged me to stop being foolish and return to my husband and do my duty. At that point, I gave up on the idea of ever repairing that relationship. I was a commodity for him to trade more so than a daughter."

"The day after tomorrow, we will visit with Helena and Blakemore for the day and then return home."

"I love you. I love you so much. I cannot even believe that I'm now free to do so," she said breathlessly.

"I love you, as well. More every day. And we have

all the time in the world to grapple with the reality of your changed station. There will be other things. Disposing of the mills and Russell's other holdings. But we'll deal with it as it comes," he promised.

They stood there for the longest time, holding one another tightly, enjoying the freedom to do so and their newfound security.

Epilogue

———————

Two Months Later

SABINE LIT the candles on the small table in her chamber. It had been laid with a small feast. It was a table set for lovers. Small plates of decadent treats that they might feed to one another, along with a large bottle of champagne. She'd dressed for the occasion or, rather, undressed for it. She wore only a silk wrapper, without even a chemise beneath it. After all, how else would one dress when informing their betrothed that they needed to hasten their wedding?

Hasten! Ha!

In the two months since they'd returned from Yorkshire, he hadn't even mentioned getting married. She simply wore his ring, lived in the house he had provided for her, and continued to serve as his mistress in every other sense. She no longer worked in her dress shop. In light of what she had thought would be her changing station, it had seemed wise to give it up. She'd allowed Bridget and Merrilee to lease it all from her, including the name, and she had even then 'invested' in the venture so that they might have the funds necessary to make it all work. Having sold off all of Russell's holdings, his debts had been satisfied, and she'd been left with a tidy sum, though not a bottomless one.

She heard the door open below stairs. He'd arrived. Rather than be seen fussing with the details, Sabine moved to one of the small chairs that flanked the fireplace and seated herself there, attempting to look casual. Moments later, when Gray entered, she greeted him with a soft smile.

"I didn't think you'd be here until later," she said.

"I was impatient to see you," he replied. "It's been too long."

A week. He'd been gone for a week. He'd been acting as her proxy to settle the last of Russell's affairs, but it was finally done. In that week while he had been away, she had made what she hoped would be a thrilling discovery.

Sabine watched as he removed his coat and moved toward the small table. He eyed the selection of foods there and then glanced up at her with one raised eyebrow.

"What is all this?"

"I believe it's called seduction," she said. "Perhaps you are unfamiliar with it from the perspective of the seduced."

His lips curved into a grin. "I'm not unfamiliar with it. I just can't imagine why you should think you would need to make such a concerted effort. You have but to crook your finger and I am at your beck and call."

"Are you?" she asked.

"You know that I am."

It wasn't exactly how she'd planned things, but if there was one thing her life on the run had taught her, it was the importance of being flexible enough to seize an opportunity. "I don't, actually. I had thought you were terribly eager to marry me. And, yet, since I have been free of my late husband and actually capable of marrying you, the subject has never come up."

He paused, with a strawberry raised halfway to his lips. "Is this your way of telling me that you wish to be married now?"

"I think it better to say that we have a very short window of time in which we can marry before our first child is illegitimate. I think somewhere in the neighborhood of six months, to be more precise on the matter."

He blinked at her for a moment. "A child? You're certain?"

"Well, as certain as I can be. I haven't had my

courses since before we left for Yorkshire. I'm terribly ill in the mornings but fine in the afternoons," she said. "It's all the classic symptoms; it just took me a bit to fully comprehend what they all meant. So, you should probably start making preparations for it—or not. Either way, I do actually need to know whether we are going to get married."

Gray put the strawberry back on the plate, wiped his hand with one of the serviettes, and walked back to the chair where he'd discarded his coat. Sabine's heart stuttered. Was he leaving? She couldn't even fathom it, but she was hardly rational at the moment, and panic was wreaking havoc on her ability to think clearly.

But he didn't leave. He simply reached inside his coat, removed a document, and brought it back to her. "I've been walking around with that in my pocket for weeks now. I obtained it the day after we returned to London and have been holding on to it with, as Mayville would put it, damnable optimism ever since."

Sabine opened the document and scanned the contents. It was a special license for the marriage of Edmund Arthur Grayson and Sally Evelyn Russell.

"How did you know my middle name?" she asked.

"That's what draws your attention? Not the fact that I've been carrying around a special license for two months?"

She laughed at that, just a bit, before growing

serious again. "Why did you wait so long? Did you have doubts?"

"Not about loving you," he answered. "Not about wanting you. But I didn't want you to feel obliged, nor did I want you to feel trapped. All you wanted was your freedom, and I couldn't bear the thought of taking it from you."

Sabine rose from her chair and draped herself about him. Her arms encircled his neck. "You are my freedom. There is no greater freedom than to be loved so completely…flaws, secrets, and all. Since you proposed the first time, I'm going to do it now. Edmund Grayson, will you marry me tomorrow morning and make an honest woman of me?"

He hugged her tightly, drawing her as close to him as possible. "Tomorrow. And the day after. And the day after that. Every day, if I could. I'll shout it from the rooftops if you will let me."

She grinned. "I'll demand it. But there's one thing you must promise me."

"And what is that?"

"The marriage license will have to say Sally and the register. But, with you, I will always be Sabine. I will always be the woman that I made myself become. The woman you helped me to become," she whispered.

"I'll call you anything you like, so long as I can call you my wife," he agreed.

"Then, take me to bed as your mistress for the very last time."

And so he did.

147

LOOK FOR LORD MAYVILLE'S STORY! Coming this September, The Plain Bride is now available for preorder at Amazon. https://amzn.to/3Aa9jni

The Plain Bride

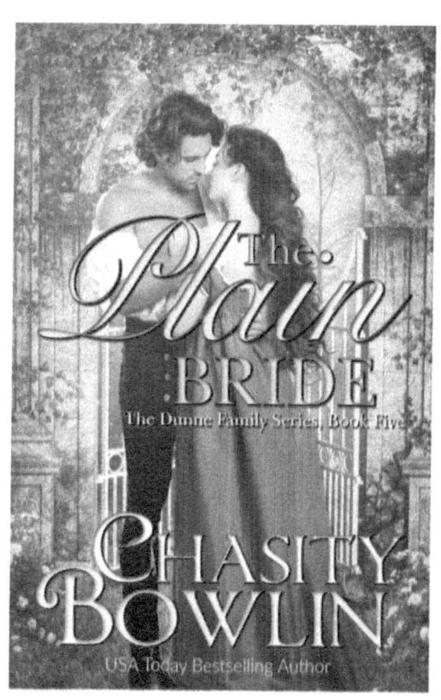

Sinclair Wortham, Lord Mayville is a man haunted by the sins of his family and by the rejection of the woman he once loved. Seeking solace from his loneliness and an escape from the secrets hidden within the crumbling walls of his family home, he heads to the local tavern for some company and truly atrocious brandy. But Sinclair makes a terrible mistake. After a brief foray outside, his drunken wandering does not lead him back to the inn and the very willing serving girl who awaits him there. It leads him, instead, to the vicarage next door... and to the vicar's plain daughter, Althea Parker.

Althea is used to being forgotten. She is used to being ignored. She is also very much used to loving Lord Mayville from afar while being utterly certain he has never glanced her way. But when he drunkenly stumbles into her bedchamber one night, she's stunned. So stunned that she screams down the rafters, bringing her father and patrons from the nearby tavern running.

Now they are trapped, forced to marry and forced to make the best of a situation that neither of them wanted—at least not in that way. But there is one universal truth... We rarely get what we want in life, but fate has a way of giving us what we need.

THE DARK REGENCY SERIES

The Haunting of a Duke

The Redemption of a Rogue

The Enticement of an Earl

A Love So Dark

A Passion So Strong

A Heart So Wicked

An Affair So Destined

STANDALONE

The Beast of Bath

Worth The Wait

THE DUNNE FAMILY SERIES

The Last Offer

The First Proposal

The Other Wife

The Late Husband

The Plain Bride (coming soon)

The Perfect Groom (coming soon)

THE LOST LORDS SERIES

The Lost Lord of Castle Black

The Vanishing of Lord Vale

The Missing Marquess of Althorn

The Resurrection of Lady

The Mystery of Miss Mason

The Awakening of Lord Ambrose

Hyacinth

A Midnight Clear

The Pirate's Bluestocking (A Pirates of Britannia Crossover)

THE VICTORIAN GOTHIC COLLECTION

House of Shadows

Veil of Shadows

Passage of Shadows

THE HELLION CLUB SERIES

A Rogue to Remember

Barefoot in Hyde Park

What Happens In Piccadilly

Sleepless In Southampton

When An Earl Loves A Governess (coming soon)

The Duke's Magnificent Obsession

The Governess Diaries

THE LYON'S DEN CONNECTED WORLD

Fall Of The Lyon

Tamed By The Lyon

THE WYLDE WALLFLOWERS

<u>One Wylde Night</u>

<u>A Kiss Gone Wylde (coming soon)</u>

<u>Too Wylde To Tame (coming soon)</u>

<u>Wylde At Heart (coming soon)</u>